Clever Way

Out

By

Raqeeb Stubbs

1

First Printing, 2020

ISBN: 9798636908197

UsWrld Publishing
122 ludlow street 1J
Newark, NJ 07114

Table of Content

About the Author

Raqeeb Stubbs aka I.b or Ibriderman is a 33 year old father, son and brother. Clever Way Out is his first book of many more to come, I.b has done over 9 years in prisons across multiple states. Now he is the CEO of UsWrld (Unite Stand With Real Life Dreams) a Organization, which aims to help children pursue their dreams. I.b also has a passion for hip hop and his own music can be heard on YouTube, soundcloud and all other platforms. Raqeeb Stubbs has no plans on stopping now yesterday past, makes tomorrow Future brighter.

 **I.B.Riderman**

 ib_riderman

Acknowledgements

First and foremost, praises and thanks to the Most High, Ahayah Ashar Ahayah, for His blessings throughout my work of this book. I would like to express my deep and sincere gratitude to my family, friends and mentors for the knowledge, inspiration.

I am extremely grateful to my mother, Sheryl for her love, prayers, and sacrifices. I am thankful to my son Avion, My sister Danielle and Brother Buck for their love, and continuing support. Also thanks to my nieces, nephews, and my late grandmother and sister.

A Special thanks goes to my friend, a great woman, who is dear to my heart Nikki for the love, positive spirit and teachings because of her I was forced to look in the mirror.

I would like to say thanks to my friends and Cover designer, for their constant encouragement. I express my special thanks to the men and women who have gone through a similar story in life as this fictional work.

Finally, my thanks go to all the people who have supported me to complete this Novel directly or indirectly.

Chapter 1

Smack, Smack, Smack! One of the robbers hits Hassan as the other one wakes his wife up to a; big ass chrome 45 in her beautiful face. "Yell, Yell, Yell" Kamela starts screaming as she sees two gunmen in her bedroom.

"Bitch shut the fuck up, that is going to only make me kill both y'all now I'm going to ask, you both two questions the truth will set you free, but lie and you die now. Question one, where is the money and Question 2, where is the drugs you only got one chance to tell the truth before my gun starts talking and he doesn't give a fuck about no answers" says the lead gunman.

Thinking of his son Clever in the other room and his wife Kamela, Hassan says "there is $100,000 under the dog house in the back yard that's all I have in the house, I don't keep drugs here I got a stash house, I can take you to get 7 birds (kilos of Cocaine) just don't kill her" Haz said trying to buy the time to come up with a way to save their lives; they came masked up so he knew they had a chance.

"Okay good job tie both they asses up and go check the dog house, the lead gunman said to his partner (Rock)

"But what about the dog" Rock said.

"I don't give a fuck shoot the motherfucker if you have to just go get the money, today payday I worked hard all week," (laugh).

While the robbers tied up Hassan and Kamela. Hassan's brain was working overtime trying to figure out where this hit was coming from one gunmen's voice sounded familiar but he couldn't place it and he always switched cars, halfway to his house to lose any tails.

His 10 year old son Clever was in his room. He was a Muslim man but had not been on his deem in a while but right now he was praying Allah would keep his son and wife safe. He wasn't afraid to die in the streets that came with the territory, that's not to say he was ready to die either, but he would not beg for his life he would welcome it like the signs saying welcome to New Jersey after many trips back and forth on the I95.

Clever had been awake when he heard the screams of his mother. He knew something wasn't right but he didn't know what it was, he was too scared to go and make any attempt to find out what was going on. Plus he thought what could he do that his father couldn't, then came the screams again he knew it was his mother and she had to be hurting badly to be screaming that loud at this time of night. He had to go see what was going on maybe he could help or maybe his father was hurt and his mother needed his help and that was why she was screaming.

As Clever got out of his bed he made sure to be very quiet the way his mother had showed him on their practice emergency drills.

He could hear her saying it, as if she was saying it right this moment, be very quiet make sure you stay quiet. First go downstairs and check the cameras in the basement, if you can make it to them. If there is a fire get out the house and call 911 if there is anything else, find me or your father but if your father and I are getting hurt call Uncle.

I never understood why she said call Uncle instead of the Police but I knew we lived a good life, better then all my friends plus I never saw my father get dressed like my friends father's I know he didn't work, so I just said okay.

Now as he got out of bed he ran to his bedroom door cracked it open as it creaked he grew more nervous, then peaked into the hallway he saw nothing. It was clear so he ran into the kitchen didn't hear the dog outside barking which was strange, because the dog would bark at the moon all night but he shrugged it off opened the door and went into the basement.

Before going down the stairs he made sure to listen he heard nothing so he proceeded to cut the lights on and close the door behind him, he was extra careful to be quiet thinking of his mother.

As he walked down the stairs he heard 3 loud bangs which made him jump, he didn't know what had just happened but it didn't sound good. As he got to the bottom of the stairs he made a right into his dad's office and then froze once he saw what was on the screen of the video camera monitors his father had installed all around the house.

There was blood everywhere in his parents room his mother and father were both tied up and bleeding badly, he was about to start crying but heard his father's voice in his head. Man up we need you then he remembered to call Uncle he was about to run up the stairs to get the phone when he saw the two masked men on the screen running to the car outside.

The smell of smoke brought him back to reality, he ran up the stairs grabbed the phone and dialed Uncle's number and told him what happened.

"Lil man get out of the house go to a neighbor's house, I'm call the Fire Department I'm on my way. Uncle Said"

Uncle jumped out of bed as he heard the news, Clever his nephew was giving him he told Gina his wife what was going on and hurriedly got dressed and ran out of the house headed to his brother's house. On the way to the car he called his right hand man Night and informed him of what was going down, Night told him he would meet him at Haz's house but Uncle told him not to there would be too many Police there.

"Just put your ear to the streets and see what we can come up with about who did this. If my brother don't make it there's going to be hell to pay on the streets of Newark." Uncle said.

Chapter 2

Uncle pulled up and saw the house was still burning, he hoped Clever had gotten out of the house. Firefighters were trying to put the blaze out but the fire was still Ablaze. Some spots were still burning crazy, "where is Clever?" Uncle yelled to the first person he saw which was a uniformed Police Officer was.

As he stopped his car just before the yellow caution tape and jumps out before anyone could stop him. The Officer was about to say something "Sir you can't park here" but as soon as heard the name he called out he stopped because he knew Detectives had been waiting for the family of the victim to arrive. He must be a member of the family or friend.

"Yes sir Clever is with the Detectives and you are" Officer Smith says putting his hand out but Uncle ignored his hand.

"I'm his Uncle, please take me to him." Uncle tells the Officer.

"Okay Sir rite this way he is with the Detectives and they would like to talk with him but they need an adult guardian's permission." The Officer stated.

"Detective Thomas, this is Clever's Uncle" the Officer say to the Detective while bringing Uncle over to them.

"Okay Officer Smith, thank you for finding him give us a minute to speak" Detective Thomas said to the Officer.

"Thank you, Officer for your help" Uncle said.

Uncle walks over to Detective Thomas.

"Hello, Sir sorry to meet under these kinds of circumstance. I am Detective Thomas of the Montclair Police Department, this is my partner Detective Roundtree we are the lead on this investigation, and you are."

"I am Rashaan Anderson, Clever's Uncle. What's going on, what happened?" He asked.

"Okay good we would like to talk to your nephew Clever, but as you know we need consent. We would like to find out what he knows, maybe he saw something or someone that can help us find out who did this to your family but we need an adult permission to speak with him. Will you give us consent to talk with your nephew?" Detective Thomas asked.

Normally Uncle didn't believe in talking to the police under any condition but he knew he had to in this situation; he wanted the police to think he wanted them to find out who did this.

"Yes Detectives you can talk with my nephew but first how are my brother and sister doing." Uncle asked

"Sorry to inform you of this but your brother had succumbed to his injuries by the time we arrived on the scene. It's unclear as to the cause of death at this time but there was an apparent gunshot wound to the Head. Your sister is in much better condition as to the fact she is still breathing. She was transported to UMDNJ (University Medical Dentistry of New Jersey) in critical condition from an apparent gunshot wound to the chest, also she has severe burns and smoke inhalation" said Detective Roundtree.

"Okay Detectives you can talk to Clever, I will be waiting for him to take him home with me." Uncle said

"This should only take 10 to 15 minutes. Here take our cards if you come up with anything helpful just give me a ring." Detective Thomas said handing over his card.

"Clever I'm going to wait in the car for you, these Officers want to ask you some questions to try and help find out what happened tonight. Go ahead and answer the questions then we can go to the hospital." Uncle said with a smile and a wink at little man knowing that was a sign he knew his brother told him as to not help the police at all.

"Okay Clever I'm Detective Thomas and this is Detective Roundtree, we are going to ask you a few questions about tonight to see if we can find out, who did this to your parents. Anything that you remember that can help us please let us know." Detective Thomas said to Clever.

"Okay sir I will do my best" Clever says in between cries and sobs.

"Clever tell us what you can remember from the time you woke up tonight" Detective Thomas asked.

"I woke up because I heard my mother screaming, she sounded scared I have never heard her scream like that before so I knew something was wrong" Clever said.

"After you heard the screams, what did you do?" Detective Thomas asked.

"Nothing at first I just hid under my covers but then I heard a few more screams and I had to go see what was going on." Clever responded.

"Okay so you went to your parents' bedroom to check on them?" Detective Thomas stated.

"No my mother always made me practice emergency safety drills in case something bad happened. So I snuck into the basement to look at the cameras." Clever told the Detective.

"Wait, wait there are cameras in the basement. What kind?" Detective Thomas asked hoping they didn't burn yet.

"Yes there are monitors to see the front yard and the backyard, plus you can see inside the house." Clever told the Detective.

"Partner get over there and let the firefighters know we need them get them cameras from the basement. See what you can come up with we need to get the videos before all the fucking water or the fire destroys them tapes. If it hasn't already I will finish up with little man." Detective Thomas tells his partner Roundtree.

"Aight cool, I'm on it." Roundtree replies.

"Okay now what happened once you got to the basement?" Detective Thomas asked Clever.

"I heard three loud bang sounds like thunder, once I got down the stairs I went to my father's office and saw my parents bleeding in their room." Clever said

"Did you see anything else little man?" Detective Thomas asked.

"Yes I saw two people running to a car waiting outside."
Clever stated starting to cry again.

"It's okay little man I'm sorry, I really am. Did you recognize the men running to the car?" Detective Thomas said to Clever.

"No Sir they had on mask, I think but it was dark couldn't really see." Clever told Thomas.

"Okay Clever what about the car did you recognize the car, what color was it?" Thomas asked.

"I don't know what kind of car it was, I just know it was black and it was big." Clever told him.

"When you say big do you mean like it was a truck? Detective Thomas asked.

"No it wasn't a truck, I mean like it was a big car with four doors not two doors." Clever said.

"Is there anything else you can remember and want to tell me, little man before we finish? Detective Thomas asked.

"No, that's all I saw Mr. Thomas." Clever said ready to go.

"Okay little man you did a good job, we are going to find the guys that did this to your parents. You can go with your uncle now, Officer Can you take this young man to his uncle over there in that silver car." Detective Thomas said to one of the Officers walking by.

Clever walked over to his Uncle's car, he saw him with his head down as he got to the car (bang, bang, bang) he hit the window three times to wake his Uncle up.

"I'm finished let's go see mommy."

"Alright little man get in we out"

Uncle wasn't sleep at all he had his head down crying it hurt to lose his brother, he was the only family he had left. Both their parents had died 2 weeks a part, 5 years ago. Now his brother was gone and he had to make sure his nephew would be good as he sat in the car trying to figure out, who had the balls to bring this move to them and at Haz house it made no sense.

They were two of the biggest and most respected hustlers in Newark plus they treated everyone with respect and made sure everybody ate. Haz used to always say if you don't feed your dogs, then they turn into wolves.

They had no beefs in the streets he could think of and this happening at Haz home didn't seem right he knew his brother was careful and would spot somebody following him. It made no sense there had to be something else maybe personal not just about the robbery.

It wasn't adding up but one thing for certain, two things for sure he would bury his brother as a true Street King, hold his nephew down as his son and make bullets rain down on the streets of Newark.

He thought as he pulled off headed for the hospital on Bergen Street. Mela you got to make it we can't lose both of y'all.

Chapter 3

"Hell yeah that's what the fuck, I'm talking about" Rock said as they pulled away from Haz's house the scene of the robbery turned murder "that was a nice Lick we got more than a hundred bandz (100,000)

"A Two5, how you know your bro was hiding the bread under the dog house" Rock asked Two5 the leader of the robbery.

"Cause that nigga used to be my right-hand man before I went in and he crossed me. We learned that from the OG Frank from down Prince Street back in the day" Two5 said.

"Oh Alright true damn I hate to be a nigga that cross you then" Rock said laughing.

"Let's go to the spot Two5, we need to split this money up part ways and get low for a while. You know that streets going to be crazy after this one" G Money the lead gunman said finally speaking thinking of Rocks fate he already knew was coming.

Two5 popped in Jay-Z's classic Reasonable Doubt CD. The lyrics cut in on the speakers with Mary J Blige singing Can't Knock The Hustle, Who Do You Think You Are? Can't Knock The Hustle,

One Day You'll Be A Star. Riding to the spot thinking of the last 10 years of his life Two5 zoned out.

10 years ago he was young getting money, in love with his high school sweetheart and on his way to being the King of Newark. Him and his girl Kamela where thinking about getting married they had their whole future in front of them, kids and the all planned the whole 9 until the night of July 20th 1999.

Tears welled up in his eyes as he thought about all he had lost over a jux and his bitch ass homie. It was supposed to be an easy lick for him, Fard and Haz.

Fard had a Jamaican Weed connect with the best Weed in the city plus he was moving major bud, so they knew he had money too. Fard knew where the Rastafarian stayed in Irvington, N.J. so the planned to rob the niggas get the money and weed that simple.

Fard was the lead man on this since he knew the Jamaicans; he put in an order of 15 pounds of Gorilla Glue Weed. Once he got inside the apartment he was supposed to text back the number of people inside the house but that text never came. We knew something was wrong once it didn't come so we had to go to plan B. Haz called Fard when he didn't pick up his phone, we knew we had to just go get him.

The plan now was to just kick in the door and start shooting first, ask questions later. When we got to the door we could hear loud noises we couldn't decipher the noise sounded like bangs but you really couldn't tell so we loaded up looked at each other and said let's go on 3.

1, 2, 3, I shot the door knob off and Haz went in first low to the floor with the AR 15, I followed behind him sending shots into the house as we got through the door. They return shots as I ducked the bullets I could see Fard tied up to the chair bleeding.

There was about two Jamaicans in the apartment I could see shooting back at me and Haz. At this time it was no longer about a robbery but a fight to not get killed and to get our homie from Fard out of there alive or at least confirm that he was dead and kill all the fucking Rastafarian motherfuckers.

Haz hit one of the shooters in the chest, he made an audible scream then fell to the floor shit was like a video game. We could hear the others shouting out gangster Jamaican shit like the movie Belly, "You come to my house try to rob me now you kill my brother you all are going to die. (Bang, Bang)

I knew those two shots was to make sure Fard was dead had to be because they didn't come our way, if Fard wasn't dead before he definitely was now. I stepped from behind the wall I was hiding behind and let off a volley of shots just as Haz let the chopper (AK-47) go turning Jamaicans shirt into a Jamaican tank top.

"Yo, Two5 we got to go man the boys (Police) going to be here in a minute if they ain't already here and I ain't going to jail for nobody. Fard my nigga but we can't just sit here and wait to go to jail, we got to go bruh." Haz said.

"What about Fard we just can't leave him here without making sure he dead" Two5 responded to Haz.

"Come on bruh you ain't stupid you heard the same shots I heard, he gone you know that Jamaican just killed him. If we don't get up out of here now we gone all be dead or in jail and that shit don't sound or look good, I am not with neither one of them options." Haz said hoping Two5 would listen because he was out either way.

He sent two shots off back at the rude boys and then took off running, "I love you Two5 but I'm out I'm not going to jail bruh, come on we can't stay no more." Haz said trying to get Two5 to come on one last time.

"I'm not leaving till I know he dead or I die we plan this together, I just can't abandon him like that" Two5 said as Haz started to make his exit.

Haz was nobody's fool he knew staying there was like suicide or turning himself in to the authorities. Haz ran back out of the building just as he got to the entrance he could hear the approaching sirens. He wouldn't be able to get back to their getaway car without the cop seeing him he figured they would be showing up in a few minutes, he couldn't get away so he did the next best thing found somewhere to hide.

He found a bando and went into the abandoned house and hid until all the commotion died down.

"This bitch ass nigga really left us." Two5 yelled out loud.

Two5 snapped out of his thoughts at least today was payback time "Yo, why y'all shoot the bitch, what happened in there? Two5 asked G-Money and Rock.

"Two5 Yo the spot right there you about to pass it, damn what you thinking about" said Rock.

"Damn, my bad I was just thinking about all this free money we about to go break up two ways" Two5 said with his gun already in his grip, spinning around in his seat pointing it at Rock.

"Rock why you shoot the female for you know it's no women or kids, bruh." Two5 said to Rock.

"I had to she heard." (Bang, Bang, Bang) the shots silenced Rock before he could finish.

"You shouldn't have done that Rock that was my heart, my love; we were supposed to be together." Two5 said to Rock's dead body.

"Yo, what you want to do with this nigga" G-Money asked Two5.

"Go open the door, I'm going to pull the car in the back, let's go split up this money then we can burn the car up, you got the gas I told you to get right." Two5 told G-Money.

Chapter 4

"Clever, I'm always going to be here for you through thick and thin. We all we got UsWrld (Unite stand with real life dreams), now before we go into this hospital I want you to know. That your mom is hurt pretty bad but we love her and Allah loves her and she is going to make it through this and come out on top." Uncle told Clever hoping and praying it was true.

"I know Uncle you got me and I got you, Lil Rah, and Tah." Clever said back to Uncle seeing the hurt in his eyes.

"Good nephew we are family now and forever, your Grandmother and Cousins are on the way up here from Florida now let's get in here and see your mom." Uncle said to him.

"Hello Sir, how can I help you" the cute receptionist with the name tag Kimberly says to Uncle.

"Yes, Hello Kimberly we are here to visit Kamela Anderson she came in about 3 hours ago." Uncle said noticing the receptionist flirting.

"Yes okay sir one second" she said as she looks to the computer screen and hits a few Keys. "Okay here it is she is in the ICU

you can visit for 30 minutes, here are your passes mister." The
receptionist said still flirting.

"Anderson, but you can't call me Rashaan." Uncle responded flirting back right now he needed something to take his mind off of what had happened.

"Okay, Mr. Rashaan take care and I hope Mrs. Anderson gets well" Kimberly said to Uncle.

"We can't stay long in her room so we going to just go in for a while, then I'm going to take you home. We both need some rest." Uncle told Clever.

They both waited for the elevator to come once it arrived Uncle pressed 4F, two doctors rode the elevator with them in a conversation about other patients or whatever doctor's talk they were having. Clever looked down and said a prayer for his mother, Allah please don't take my mother, I love her, I need her please let her live my father's already gone if I lose her all I would have left is uncle. I love him but he's not mommy praise Allah.

As the elevator stopped Clever felt a little better. Once they got off of the elevator in the waiting room they could see Nicki and Tonya, Mela's best friends. They were like Clever's Aunts he was glad to see them, upon seeing Clever and Uncle they rushed over to Clever giving him hugs and kisses.

"Hey baby you okay baby (kiss, kiss, kiss, kiss, cry, cry)

Uncle could tell they were both hurting for their friend but we're trying to stay strong for Clever. "Hello ladies, how is she" Uncle asked them breaking up their session will Clever.

"She still alive but other than that she's pretty fucked up, doctors won't let us stay in their but 15 minutes everything is touch-and-go right now it's up to her to keep fighting to live." Tonya said to Uncle giving him a hug.

As they entered the room the smell of the fire was still in the air but that didn't even bother Uncle but when he saw all the machines Mela was hooked up to that caught him off guard.

Tubes, machines, noises, IVs running everywhere it looked like a scene from a Frankenstein show he was waiting for someone to yell it's alive or some shit. By the look of her you would think she was dead already or at least think how could she not be dead yet. The fire had left her with severe burns from head to toe and the wounds were too fresh to be wrapped up. So, what she look like was a giant beef jerky.

"Clever I'm going to step out of the room and let you talk to your mother for a while. Kamela, I know you can hear me we are here for you this is your brother Rah and your son Clever. Cut your lights back on and come back to us it's not time, we love you, and we need you." Uncle said as a single tear fell down his face. "Okay Clever I'll be outside waiting with your aunts.

As Uncle left out of the room door he bumped it to Jahmela, Clever's Aunt on her way to the see her sister. "Hold on Jah let little man get a minute with his mother they both need it right now." Uncle said to her.

"Okay Rah" Jahmela said being one of the only people to still call him anything but Uncle. "How is she?"

"Not good at all right now we both know she is a fighter though, if anybody can pull through she can. She going to make it shit she ain't got a choice" Uncle said more hoping than believing. "You talk to your mother yet."

"Yeah her and my cousin's will be up here in the morning their plane scheduled to land at 10:38 at JFK" Jahmela told Uncle.

"Okay, I'm going to send them a car in the morning or go myself, I need to get some rest let me get Clever, We will see you later Jah" Uncle said hugging Jahmela.

Chapter 5

Clever pulls up a nearby chair and begins to pay a Muslim prayer. His father taught him many times over "In the name of Allah, Get rid of the hardship and heal, O Lord of the People, you are the Healer, and there is no healing of disease like yours. Let it be healing that is not betrayed by sickness."

Jahmela enters the room but freezes upon realizing Clever is praying, she stops and tears come to her eyes, she begins to recite the prayer with her nephew.

"Thee do we serve and thee do we beseech for help, Guide us on the right path, the path of those upon whom thou hast bestowed favors, not of those upon whom thy wrath is brought down, nor of those who go Astray. Allah is the great only he can save your mother, I love you Allah Akbar the both said in unison upon hearing that Clever turned around and saw his aunt with tears in her eyes and ran over to her. "Hey auntie, its ok Allah knows best he is the ruler and he will save mommy. We can't say the same about the people who did this I know uncle will get them or I will get them one day.

Jahmela looked at her 10 year old nephew and didn't know what to say but one thing she did notice was he meant every word. She was watching him go from the smart sweet kid to a cold, cold young man in this cold, cold world right in front of her face. Don't worry about anything like that Clever we love and care for you just as your parents do. Grandma and Cousin Ray will be here in the morning, so go on with uncle and get some rest she kissed her nephew, I will see you later. I love you

Okay auntie, I love you too.

Chapter 6

"Aye girl we out if you need us you know our numbers"
said Tonya and Nicki.

"Okay, girl I'm going to stick around a little while longer see who else shows up here love y'all be safe" Jahmela said.

After her home girls left she went to get something to eat, she found the cafeteria on the first floor ordered a chicken salad and coffee she sat down, but couldn't eat, all she could do was think of her past, her present, and her future how could this happen.

She still had her and Mela's two best friends from high school and her kids, other than that she had lost so much. Now here they were her only sister was fighting for her life, her homeboy, Kamela's husband and Rashaan her first love's brother was dead. She thought back to when it all went wrong.

She was about to graduate high school her and Rah were in love she had just found out she was pregnant only a few weeks but she was extremely happy, nobody knew yet but Kamela.

She was definitely going to keep the baby, she knew her father would be mad but he would get over it and Rah would be so happy they would finally be a family. She would go to Essex County College it would be hard but she could do it, then she got the call from Kamela.

"Girl Two5 got locked up, they tried to rob them Jamaican's in Irvington word is Fard got killed, and some witness said it was 3 of them, now the police looking for the last suspect" Mela said.

"I hope dummy wasn't with them damn dumb ass niggas let me cut on the news hold on girl, they saying something about it on Channel 7" Breaking News 3 arrested and 3 dead in a daring home invasion in Irvington, N.J. Kevin Lockett, Jamik Rutledge, Terry Ally, where all arrested on counts of Murder, Robbery, Assault, and Burglary. The names of the dead are not being released until the families are notified, back to you Alicia.

"Oh, damn girl at least they got all the robbers fucked up they got Two5, I need Rah girl the baby might slow his ass down I'm sorry about Two5 though he will be alright he a strong dude" Jahmela said thankful she didn't here Rah's name, she never liked Two5 so she really could careless she thought it probably better for her sister he was caught.

"But naw girl they didn't catch all the robbers cause Fard dead, I think they just locked up Two5 and probably 2 of the Jamaican's" Mela said.

"Oh okay, girl let me call Rah" Jahmela said. This just in ABC News lives Downtown Newark, N.J. Another suspect has just been apprehended in the Irvington home invasion Rahsaan Anderson has been charged with Robbery, Murder, Assault, and Burglary. He is currently being booked in and scheduled for Arraignment Monday morning. "No, No, No could be heard screaming through the entire house." "Jahmela, Jahmela, Jahmela, Kamela yelled through the phone "I'm on my way."

Jahmela cried the whole weekend on her sisters shoulders "what am I going to do Kamela, I'm pregnant, in school and my child's father is in jail why, why god."

"Listen girl shut the fuck up we gone go down there Monday and see about our men, that's all that we can do" Kamela said. After that Jahmela didn't shed another tear until Monday came, they got up bright and early they arrived at the courthouse on 50 W. Market 9:00am Sharp to their surprise Hassan, Rah's brother was there already,.

"What's up, Haz" said Kamela.

"Shit got to see what's up with my bruhs" he said with a wink to Kamela, He had always liked Kamela but she was with Two5.

"Oh okay come on you two let us get up the stairs before they see the Judge" Jahmela said pushing Haz.

She wasn't crazy she saw him flirting with her sister; she thought damn niggas ain't shit Two5 only been gone 3 days, little did she know him and Mela had been fucking around for a while, plus Two5 wasn't really his man that was his brother's boy that's how they locked his brother up. The witness identified him because him and Rah looked almost like twins and everybody knew if they saw Two5 then Rah was somewhere around.

"Kevin Lockett you are being charged with 2 counts of first degree Murder, 2 counts of second degree Aggravated Assault, 1 count of first degree Armed Robbery, and 2 counts of second degree Possession of a weapon/Firearm your bail will be set at $5 million, If you can make bail you are to keep in contact with your lawyer until your court date is scheduled, if not you will remain in custody" The Judge Informed the defendant.

"Damn" somebody in the audience said a little too loud for the judges liking "Order, Order, Next is Rashaan Anderson." Rah Public Defender said to speak "Your Honor my client plea is not guilty, he has no record and was not found on the scene, we ask for a minimal bail." "Mr. Anderson I see you have no record which is a good thing but due to the nature of the charges against you the bail is at $1 million dollars, next." The judge stated to Rah moving on the next case.

"Baby, we are going to find a way to get you out" Kimela yelled "Yeah Bruh We got y'all" Haz said also. "Bailiff, get these people out of my courtroom, now before I start sending people to jail for the night" the Judge order.

Chapter 7

Uncle woke up a few hours later on the couch in the den; he cut the news on and went to his master bedroom to take a shower. He knew he had a long day ahead of him. He wanted to get his ear to the streets early but first he needed a shower, upon stepping in his room he saw his beautiful wife laying in the bed. He went over and kissed her, she woke up instantly "hey baby you okay, how bad is it" she asked.

"Bad bae Haz dead and Mela burned, bad she is in a fight for her life" Rah said.

"How is Clever doing I know he going through a lot", Gina Uncle's wife said.

"Yeah he is but he a strong kid, he gone be alright I got a lot to do today so I'm going to leave him here with you and the boys, can you take off today." Uncle said.

Gina Laughed "I better be able to take off, we own the agency" Uncle smiled after all that went on last night he forgot that .

"Okay, bae I'm going to get in the shower" Uncle said.

As soon as he stepped in the bathroom Gina got out of bed went to check on the boys, they were still sleeping good she thought let me go make some breakfast. As soon as she got downstairs she could hear the news 1 killed, she ran to the TV to find out more information on what had happened 1 killed, 1 injured in a suspicious house fire in Montclair, N.J.

Firefighters were called to the scene around 11:30pm last night upon entry into the home they came upon to 2 badly burned bodies; police are investing as we speak. Back to you Alicia, reporting live from Montclair, N.J. This is A.J. Ross.

As Uncle sat under the hot shower water his brain went back to Jahmela, damn she looked good he kind of missed her, seeing her brought him back to the days they were in love.

He was back in his cell in the Essex County Correctional Faculty on the 12th floor, his Bunkie was some ole head from Hawthorne name Zeke, he use to always say young'un, you gone be alright them crackers ain't got shit. He knew that because he Rah really didn't do it but he still had a million dollar bail with no way out plus he still didn't see Two5.

They had been in the building 2 weeks, it came to his mind maybe Two5 was snitching but he would have to wait to see, Jahmela was holding him down every visit, money everything, she told him his brother was fucking with Mela now but he didn't care he just wanted to go home.

"Anderson Pack it up" the C.O yelled

"Why were I'm going" Uncle asked.

"I don't know they said pack it up you moving" the C.O. told him.

"Aight young'un be safe, here's my info holla at me let me know what's what" his Bunkie said.

"Aight, OG I got you one love be safe" Rah said giving the OG dap.

"Anderson, come on you going to the 11th floor" the C.O. yelled out.

When Rah got to the 11th floor shit was like the wild, wild, west the bloods had just come to Jersey but they were running shit on the 11th floor. On the 12th there wasn't really any gang shit going on but down here it seemed like everybody was banging some kind of set. Rah didn't give a fuck but he knew he had to watch them niggas.

"Yo Rah, what's good bruh I missed you been trying to get you down here." Rah heard the voice and turned around he knew it had to be Two5.

"What's good bruh, oh you got me moved I ain't know what the fuck was up," Rah said.

"What cell they got you in 9 top right" Two5 asked.

"Yeah that where they got me at who they nigga in that cell"
Rah said.

"You good in there that's my dude he real stand up nigga, lol
naw that's my cell go put your shit up in the cell we gone kick it but let
me get back to this poker game got that bread on the line, love that
nigga." Two5 said leaving.

As Rah was making the top bunk Two5 came in the room with
a pillow case full of food and cigarettes. "Damn Two5, I see nothing
changed you still gambling like a motherfucker." Rah said.

"Yeah nigga you know me I will bet my life I guess I got a
gambling problem. You already know Two5 gotta eat plus these niggas
sweet as bear meat bruh. But yo let me put you up on a few things, this
tier on some super blood shit you ain't banging me either so you
already know we gotta always watch our backs, you my nigga so you
already know I got you. My brother down with these blood niggas he
supposed be one of the top niggas so we good for now but always
watch your front and back. You watch me I watch you Rah but on
another note what's good with your bail," Two5 said.

"You already know shit fucked up they got niggas at ransom
can't make a million dollar bail just like you can't make that 5 million.
Haz got me a lawyer I think he got you one too, so what really
happened I'm hearing it was you Fard, and Haz made the move I

saying I'm rolling with y'all I ain't do shit but we gone rock out my guy." Rah said

"Truth be told we made a move Fard got killed, your brother did the smart thing got low and I got caught fucked up you sitting here for this shit but we gotta handle it. Yea, bruh I messed up Haz told me to leave when he dipped" Two5 said.

"Hold up, Hold up you saying Haz left you behind" Rah asked.

"Yea bruh he left us but he was supposed to leave us Fard was already dead and we were just sitting there waiting to die or be in here if we stayed I fucked up and look what happened we in here and he out there. I heard he fucking with Mela the streets talking, I mean she come see me and put bread on my books but I can see it all in her eyes she look happy its cool thought he paid for my lawyer the least he could do" Two5 said that out loud but deep down he was on fire Haz would pay one day, he would never turn snitch but he would get him back.

"Rah I ain't gone let you go down with me on my shit but you gone have to ride with me until I get a good deal, but I'm going to cut you loose in the end facts" Two5 spoke them words with nothing but the truth in his heart.

"Kevin Lockette you are a very lucky man today, you were facing a very lot of time in prison but due to the plea agreement your

Attorney and the Prosecutor have worked out you will only be sentenced to 12yrs with mandatory %85 to be served. You will be granted 408 days jail credit, your co-defendant Rashaan Anderson's charges will be dismissed due to your testimony." Bang, Bang the Judge bangs the gavel "Next Malik White."

Just as Two5 said he would do over a year earlier, he took the charges Rah was a free man and ready for the world. A lot had changed for him in the year plus, he and Jahmela were not together anymore she tried to hang on but once she had the miscarriage Rah couldn't make it work any longer he truly thought she had an abortion. Haz and Mela had welcomed a brand newborn son into the world his nephew Clever Anderson.

Chapter 8

"Kids wake up breakfast is ready" Gina yelled.

They all came running to the kitchen "Good Morning mommy, Hey Auntie" they all said in unison.

"Tah go get your father and tell him breakfast is ready."

"Okay mommy" Tah ran upstairs "Daddy, Daddy" he stopped when he got to the door, he saw his father cleaning a gun. Bang, Bang he knocked on the open door, "daddy mommy said come eat the food done."

"Aight lil man I'm on my way down" Rah said tucking his gun.

When he got downstairs he kissed his wife, patted the boys on the head told his wife he had to go hit the streets he need to get information on what really happened last night. "Clever your grandmother will be here in about 2 hours see you later" Uncle ran outside jumped in his BMW 650 called his right hand man, Night train told him to meet him on Avon and Treacy Ave.

When Uncle pulled up, Night was already there waiting for him being as his ride was only a few minutes away and Uncle had a 30 plus minute ride.

"What's good? Bruh" Night asked Uncle

"I don't even fucking know, Night shit crazy Mela fighting for her life, Haz dead, I don't know what to do but I do know one thing we gone find out. What the fuck really going on out here, first thing first let's see what Tesha nosy ass know, she hit my phone this morning said she heard a few things." Uncle said to Night.

Knock, Knock, Ding Dong!! "Tesha open the fucking door it's me Uncle."

"Okay, boy hold on I'm coming down now, damn nigga." Tesha opened the door a few seconds later looking good enough to eat in some boy shorts and a tank top. "Hey Fellas what's up"

"Tesha Damn girl I wasn't hungry before but I could eat now" Night said.

"Boy shut up"

"I'm just saying you looking good boo" Night said smiling.

"Enough with all that flirting and shit" Uncle said as they made their way upstairs to Tesha's apartment. "Tesha what's good, you called me what you know about the shit that went down last night, I hope you got some good shit."

"Well I don't know if it can help or if it's even important but Rock said" Tesha said.

"Hold up Tesha who fuck is Rock" asked Uncle.

"You know Rock, Uncle he went to school with us but anyway, I been dealing with him a while now he always be a broke small time hustling nigga but lately he been moving out spending crazy bread so I asked him one day. What he been doing what's his new hustle he said ain't nothing changed he just finally got back right, some shit about being on the block again. So I let it go but then he gave me $6,000 said go shopping for myself and the kids. Now I know him and this ain't seem right, I mean I spent it but" Tesha said.

"Hurry up damn get to the information already" Night said.

"Okay, okay so I followed him one night to some building on 11th street, he me that nigga G-money and some other dude I don't know but I overheard them talking about a robbery that would be a big lick, then I saw the new about Haz and I called you" Tesha said finally finished.

"Okay Tesha good looking here take this for your help (Uncle gave her $2,000 for her info, he didn't know if it would help yet but it was a start) good looking Ma we out if you see Rock don't say nothing to him about nothing" said Uncle.

Uncle and Night both walked down the stairs to their cars, both thinking about what Tesha had just told them.

"Good look Night! I'm out but I'm ah holla at you later tonight, put your ear to the streets, see what they talking about if you hear anything hit my jack"

"Aight my boy" Night said giving Uncle a handshake and hug.

Uncle had forgot to set up a ride for Clever's Grandmother and it was too late now, her plane had arrived at JFK airport 20 minutes ago he knew she wouldn't be mad she always liked him.

He called Jahmela (Ring, Ring) Hello the voice on the other end said, "yeah Jah I forgot to send a car for your mother can you tell her just get in a cab from the airport" Uncle asked.

"Don't worry about it when I didn't hear from you this morning I handled everything, they are on their way to the hospital now" Jahmela told Uncle.

"Okay thanks Jah; I will meet y'all at the hospital I might have some information about what happened you can help me understand." Uncle said before hanging up.

They met up at the hospital about an hour later, Uncle had to go pick up Clever and when he got there little Rah and Tah wouldn't let him leave without them going too. Come on boys lets go upstairs "Rah,

Rah" someone was yelling his name when he turned around he saw the face behind the voice it was Mela's cousin Ray.

"What's good, Rah what it do cuzzo" he said to Clever giving him and the boys some dap. "Rah I need to holla at you A.S.A.P"

"Aight Ray let's take the boys upstairs then we can kick it." Uncle said.

They all went into the hospital got there visitors passes, Kimberly the cute receptionist from yesterday gave them there passes all smiles. When they got upstairs Uncle saw the same faces from yesterday plus Jahmela and Kamela's mother Crystal, today seemed more upbeat and less somber than yesterday.

"Hey everybody what's going on you guys looking uplifted" Uncle asked. *Crystal spoke first "yeah the Doctors say Kamela has a good chance to make it now it's just up to her, she's still in the Coma but their optimistic she will pull through."*

"Okay that's great news need that right now" Ray said.

"Hey grandma Clever said giving her a hug." (Rah and Ray stepped off to talk.) Grandma I missed you glad to see you now let's go see mommy."

"Yea, Ray what's going on" Uncle asked

"You know how I get down and that's family in there and your brother was my man, shit I like him more than I like you" (laughs)

"But on a serious note I know you got your ear to the streets my nigga and if you riding then I want in, nothing more nothing less!" Ray said to Rah ready to go to war. He didn't have any parents his mother died giving birth and his father was a junky all he had was Kamela, Jahmela and Aunt Crystal.

"Alright Ray you already know you got it give me your number and keep your phone on and I might have some move tonight. Now let's get in this room I need to holla at Jah, also, but you definitely in on any move" Rah said

As they entered Mela's room, Lil Rah was reading a prayer. "Allah knows best please help my aunty get up and her please!" They stopped to join in on the prayer. When Lil Rah was finished, uncle said Jahmela I need to talk to you and Ray, but first Crystal let's step out the room so I can talk to you. (Crystal and Rah left the room)

"How are you handling everything" uncle asked.

"I'm alive and well best I can be Rah under these circumstances" Crystal spoke

"Okay I'm just asking because a lot is going on, we don't know about and I got to get to the bottom of this. How long you staying up here?" Rah asked

"I don't know yet as long as I can I guess your brothers funeral, see if Mela comes out of her coma, and Clever going to have to get him situated." Crystal said.

"Okay, good I know Clever your grandson but I will keep him with me I already got two boys I can handle one more" (yeah, yeah but not the wife as she laughed) They both Laughed.

"Okay Rah I'm with you were going to have to do everything as a team me, you and Jahmela." Crystal said

"Ray exited the room, Aye yo Ray tell Jahmela to come out with you I need to talk to both y'all about a few things" Ray heard Rah and stepped back in the room to get Jahmela.

Crystal gave Jah a look but said nothing. "Aight Rah talk to you later" she said getting up "let me get back in there."

When Ray and Jahmela exited the room, Rah met them "let's go downstairs and talk in a cigarette for real."

They made their way to make down the stairs and out the building let's take a walk and talk Rah announced.

Rah lit a Newport and began walking towards South Orange Ave.

"Okay now here's what I got as of now, a female I know said she been fucking with some broke nigga name Rock from the

Vailsburg section. She said I went to school with the nigga. I was wondering do one of y'all know the nigga?"

Ray spoke first "I remember son a little bit he used to be fucking with the nigga Ty Black and boy Rock fell off."

"Jahmela you used to talk to Mela all the time did she mention any threats or crazy shit going on?" Uncle asked

"Nah Rah the only thing she would say was that Haz was mad, a lot somebody was stealing and y'all couldn't figure out who was doing it. Oh yeah she said somebody would call her cell phone and say creepy shit like hey baby what you got on, always on a different number and she tried to trace the calls they came back to pay phones in Atlanta so she left it alone." Jahmela said.

"Do you think she told Haz" Rah asked.

"No I don't know but I think she didn't want to bother him with it" Jahmela said.

"Aight all we got to do now is get this Rock nigga and Ty black, Jahmela I need you to get me some information on these cats, addresses numbers where they be at, whatever you can come up with." Rah told her

"Okay Rah I wasn't planning on going to work today but I will do a quick drop in at the court building and see what I can get." Jahmela said.

Jahmela was the head public defender in the municipal courthouse "I will call you in about an hour with all the info."

"Aight, Clever and my boys going to go with your mother, I'm out got to put my ear on the streets and do me. Ray I'm hit your jack later once I see how this move be." Rah said I'm out hugging Jahmela.

Chapter 9

Rah left the hospital room and went straight to the block. He still had money to pick up and he still had to re-up to put work on a few of his and Haz blocks, first stop was a building on Osbourne Terr. and Clinton Ave.

He pulled into the back parking lot jumped out and walked to the apartment door gave 4 knocks, stop followed by 2 more to let Milly and Lockout know it was him at the door.

Lockout opened the door "what's good big bruh, what it do?"

"Shit just coming to the hood to get that bread!" he said with authority

"Aight it's right there." Lockout said.

Cool where Milly at? Rah asked.

"He on the block, we heard what happened he off his shit he said he need to find out something about what happened." Lockout said.

"Good look let me know if anything pops up if y'all need any work let me know show still go on, still got money to make. Uncle said to Lockout

"Aight Rah you already know be easy big bruh!" Lockout said dapping Uncle.

Uncle went to make a few more pickups at his and Haz spots. He had to go back and get a few packages to drop off for a couple his people's re-ups.

"Before the last pickup, he got a call from Jahmela "Hello yeah Rah I got some of that information for you I couldn't come up with an address for Rock but I got his real name Jamal Ware. His known affiliates are Latesha Smith, Tyreke Thomas aka Ty Black. Latesha's last known address is." Jahmela was saying.

Rah interrupted Jahmela before she could finish "I already know about Tesha" Uncle said.

"Oh Okay well onto Ty, he just came home from down Bayside his parole address is 79 Sunset Ave in Vailsburg he doesn't have any job I could find. He has 2 daughters one is 4 years old, the other is 7 years old they're both with their mother Alicia Williams her address is 164 Riverside Court in Newark that's down by Grafton Ave that's it Rah" Jahmela finished giving Uncle all the information she found out.

"Okay, Jahmela good job thank you love one last thing how are you holding up?" Uncle asked.

"I'm holding Rah; I'm taking it one day at a time." Jahmela said answering Rah's question.

After Uncle hung up he called Milly and Lockout told them to be on the lookout for Ty Black and Rock, to call him he they saw or heard anything.

"Don't hurt them if you see them just watch them for now" Uncle said.

Then he called Night and Ray told them he got that information and to meet him at A&R's at 10 pm.

"Oh and Night bring out the van" Uncle told them. (The van was an all-black conversion van with 2 stash boxes big enough to hide a body or whatever else needed to disappear.) Uncle called Tesha (Ring, Ring, Ring)

"Hello what up Uncle?" Tesha asked.

"Do you know Ty Black" Uncle asked Tesha.

"Yeah I know him that was Rock's man before he got locked up" Tesha said.

"Okay do you know where he at now?" Uncle asked.

"Not really but I know he came home a couple of months ago. I remember Rock said they was hustling again back on their old block I think." Tesha told Uncle.

"What was their old block" Uncle asked.

"I'm not sure but I know it's up on Springfield Ave, I think its 20th or 21st Streets somewhere over that way." Tesha told Uncle everything she knew.

"Okay thanks Tesha you a lifesaver" (Rah laughed because if the information Tesha was providing him was good it would be the exact opposite of life saving) Bye they both said before hanging up.

Uncle pulled up to the bar dressed in a casual outfit, black True Religion jeans, a gray button up shirt and some Prada shoes. The bar meet up spot served to purposes first the music would make it hard to be heard you never knew who was listening and there would be plenty of people there that could say he was at the bar all night if the need ever arrived. Ray showed up 10 minutes after Uncle, he ordered a Jack and Coke once he found Uncle at the bar sipping a drink.

"What's good Cuzzo" Ray said to Rah giving him some dap.

"Shit bruh waiting on my man Night to get here in next 20 minutes or so, so just enjoy yourself don't get drunk thought we got a lot to discuss but have yourself a good time" Uncle said.

Uncle mingled with associates, friends and other people he knew while he waited the 20 minutes for Night, this was a custom they did anytime they had to put in work be seen a while at a local bar or somewhere in public then go handle business. Tonight would be no different, Night arrived exactly 20 minutes later dressed to party he parked the van around the corner as to not be seen in it just in case.

Night walked in saw Uncle at the back table, he went over "What's good bruh, what it do" Night said.

Uncle Called Ray over to the table "Yo Ray, Ray, come here!"

"Who the fuck is this nigga Rah you already know I ain't off no new Niggas" Night said to Rah about Ray.

"Naw he good, he family he Mela cousin I have known son a long time plus he my brother's man and he want sauce" Uncle spoke to Night "He good, he a shooter." Night looked up to see Ray coming to the table.

"What's good bruh? Ray asked walking up to the table.

"I'm Gucci bruh" Night said to no one in particular.

"Night this Ray, Ray this Night" Uncle said introducing everyone. Uncle spoke from here on out both of them listened "Here's what's up I got some information on the Nigga Rock as of now he a ghost but his man be up on 20th Street, Nigga name Ty Black. Uncle said informing Ray and Night what he knew.

"Aight I know son he just came home matter fact I seen the nigga a couple of days ago" Night told them.

"Okay good then we gone go through there buy some bally in Ray's rental if we see the nigga out there we gone snatch his ass up, plain and simple Ray you jump out the back of the van and if the nigga try to run then shoot him. Night you know him so you ride in the passenger seat but you gotta get him to come to the passenger side so we can make it easier to snatch him up, it's probably gone be niggas on the block strapped up so when Ray grab the nigga, Night you get out with the chopper to make sure we leave the block same way we came" Uncle give all instruction on the plan now it was go time.

They all got up paid there tabs and left the bar leaving Uncle's car out front and jumping into Ray's rental.

"Night where is the van at" Uncle asked.

"Go straight then make a right and another right you will see it on the corner" Night told Ray who was driving.

When they got to the van Uncle said to Ray let go change, they all got in the back of the van got dressed up in all black checked their weapons in the stash box and where ready to ride.

"Night follow us we going to all jump in the rental once we get around the corner from 20th on 18th street" Uncle said. Uncle and Ray jumped into the rental and pulled off, followed by Night.

Once they go to 18th street Night parked the van and got into the rental car with them, they made a right onto 20th street they saw about 10 dudes out there hustling but none of them was Ty Black as they keep riding they saw him further down the block making a sale.

"Jackpot there he go right there" Night said from the backseat.

"Aight Ray pull up to him" Uncle said let me get 5 dimes passing Ty Black a $50 Ty put the weed in Uncle's hand. "Aight bruh good look you got a number I can hit you when I'm through again. Uncle said.

"Yeah 973-847-5555" Ty Black said as Uncle put the number into his phone.

"What's your name? Bruh" Uncle asked.

"Ty Black" Ty said.

"Aight bruh I'm ah hit you up when I need more." Uncle said as Ray pulled off.

Ray circled the block pulled behind the van everybody got out of the rental and headed for the van. After they go into the van they went over the plan one last time, Uncle was driving Night was in the passenger seat and Ray in the back everybody got their guns ready and they pulled off.

As they turned the corner of 20th street, they spotted Ty Black he ran to Nights window. Perfect Ray thought "How many you want, ole shit what's good my boy" Ty said when we saw Night. Ty put his arm in the window to shake Nights hand as if on cue Ray was out of the side door grabbing Ty Black up like a rag doll.

"Come on my boy we got a lot of catching up to do" Night said to Ty Black.

And like that Ty Black was in the back of the van with Ray knocked out from the gun butt to the back of his skull. Everything went off without a hitch nobody saw a thing.

Chapter 10

"What's good? Bruh" G-money said to Two5 over the phone. "I need to holla at you, I got another move to make and I could use your assistance on this one" Two5 thought about what G-money was asking him for about a minute or two then said alright. "Two5 meet me at Margaritas' in an hour we can get some breakfast and talk." G-money said.

As Two5 sat there after the conversation he had just had with G-money his mind started back to the past life and what could have been, he heard Mela would survive but that ship had sailed.

"Yo, G-money before I shot Rock he was about to say something what was he trying to say how shit went down inside there" Two5 asked.

"She heard my name the stupid nigga called me G-money in there so Rock shot he for his fuckup, dude was dead regardless but that's why he shot her." G-money told Two5.

"Well it is what it is now but definitely he had to go" Two5 said.

Coming out of his daydream Two5 got dressed and headed out of the hotel on the highway U.S. 1 & 9 headed towards Central Ave. He arrived at Margaritas 25 minutes later just as he saw G-money getting out of a Silver Chrysler 300. (Beep, Beep, Two5 hit the horn so G-money could see him and then found a parking spot.)

"What's good? G-money racks I see that bitch right there she still looking good as a motherfucker" Two5 said giving G-money the customary dap and hug.

Yeah you already know Two5, I got to keep my bitches looking good my guy, it ain't right if nobody else ain't watching her while she with you" G-money said laughing.

They both walked in laughing went to the counter and placed there orders Two5 said 'let me get some home fries, beef sausage, scrambled eggs, cheese grits and orange juice."

G-money said "damn nigga you ordering half the restraint but that shit sounds good let me get the same thing mama but instead of sausage let me get beef bacon."

"Alright Papi you can have a seat we will bring your food to you when it is ready" the older Spanish lady who took their orders said.

They picked a table in the back and sat down to start their conversation while they waited for their orders.

"Yeah bruh shit gone get hot about that move we made good thing is ole boy gone one less worry, but on another note I heard that nigga Ty Black got snatched off of 20th street last night." G-Money said.

"Wait, wait who the fuck is Ty Black and how the fuck his get snatched up, who the hell out here moving like that and what that got to do with us" Two5 said questioning G-Money. (Their food was brought to their table and they started eating.)

G-money continued "Ty Black is one of Rock's boys they used to get money together before Ty Black got bagged he did 5 years, he just came home last month, niggas on the block saying dudes jumped out of a black conversion van put a gun to his head an forced son in the back of the van then pulled off. So I'm figuring niggas must've got a line on Rock but couldn't find him so they grabbed up his man to see if he got in information, I don't know if Rock was talking to Ty Black about us but niggas definitely know I fuck with Rock a little bit so I just want to put you up on game."

"Aight bruh! True, True I don't really know what to tell you cause to tell the truth, I don't give a fuck about the nigga Rah, Uncle or whatever he calling himself now or any of his soldiers I'm with whatever bruh. I'm about to go back to Atlanta, I got an infant son. I'm good down there got a whole family I just came back up here to make that move with y'all and its done now.

So I'm out, I would offer you the opportunity to come with me its crazy money down there but I know you not running from nobody. So I'm not even going to disrespect you but what I will say is take you and wifey on a vacation for a little while enjoy the spoils of your labor, let the heat die down then pop back up and see what the lick read." Two5 finished.

"Yeah bruh that's a good idea I think I'm going to do that, cause I was about to just go at them niggas guns blazing but you right plus the nigga Ty Black might not know shit about us or that could be something else totally" G-money said.

"Aight my nigga stay up be on point, when you leaving thou" G-money asked.

"I'm supposed to be out tomorrow night" Two5 really was leaving in about 3 hours but he didn't want G-money knowing all his business you could never let the right hand knowing, what the left hand was doing.

"Aight bruh I love that nigga," G-money said. (Pulling out his cell phone Ring, Ring, Bae pack your shit we going to the Dominican Republic.)

G-money's girl dropped the phone as she started screaming, she was more than excited and went straight to packing her clothes forgetting he was even on the phone, G-money just looked at the phone smiling and got into his car and pulled off.

Chapter 11

"Wake this bitch ass nigga up, better not start that crying shit again this time I'm going to shoot his ass not just clunk him in the head" Ray said Night started laughing (Smack, Smack, Smack, Smack)

"Damn you hit that nigga hard as hell he still ain't waking up get that bucket right there" Uncle said Rah was in his zone he fell in love with this murder game after he shot his wife's uncle for raping her, when they were in high school that was the reason people in the streets started calling him Uncle anyway. "Yo, throw that ice on this nigga that should wake his ass up" Uncle told Ray.

Ray dumped the ice on Ty Black and instantly he woke up like somebody cut the lights on (he was shivering but managed to ask them who the fuck where they and what beef they had with him.)

"Shut the fuck up with the 21 questions, Nigga I ask the questions in here you answer right and you get to see another day on this earth are we clear" Uncle said.

Ty said yes we clear, "So you don't know me well let me introduce myself and my partners well I'm Uncle this man right here is my main man Night and the guy right there Is my cousin

64

Ray, Now I have some good news for you my man Night say's you are a stand up dude so there is a chance you can walk out of this place alive and well it's all up to you my man.

Now here is how this game right here is going to go I'm going to ask you some questions there won't be any torturing of you or none of that type shit this ain't a hood book. But for every question I ask you I want one answer the truth that's it that's all if think you lying my man Ray gone shoot your stupid ass so I advise you tell the truth and if I don't get what I came for then you already know what is . Good Night."

Ty Black sat there his hand and head where both hurting he was tied to a chair scared shitless as if he was about to meet his maker to atone for all of his past sins, he prayed if he made it out of this situation he would get his life together no more hustling none of that shit.

Uncle asked the first question "Where is your man Rock?"

Ty answered that without a problem "I don't know man I ain't seen him in a while I been trying to get in touch with son for few days ain't heard shit from him (Bang Uncle shot him in the leg) I swear I ain't seen him the nigga owe me money I hope you get him so I can get my money from that fool."

(Bang) Uncle shot him again in the arm this time "Nigga you think I'm playing with your ass got to think I'm playing" Uncle said out of pure rage.

"Naw, Naw bruh I'm not playing with y'all, I ain't seen Rock in a minute on my mother man I ain't seen him." Ty Black said pleading his case not trying to get shot again.

"Alright my man next question do you know anything about a robbery that took place few days ago, I got reason to believe you and your boy Rock robbed my brother and killed him who sent y'all?"

"It wasn't me ain't rob nobody I ain't into that robbery shit since I been home I just been hustling weed up on 20th bruh this all I do, I don't know what Rock done did but I don't got shit to do with nothing." Ty black said scared shitless now more than ever.

(Bang) Ray shot him again this time in his other arm Ty Black howled like a wolf he was losing a lot of blood about ready to faint.

"Nigga you got one more chance or it's good night fuck it, you better answer this question with the truth and nothing but the truth or so help you god, it's going to be your last nap, Rock your man right but would he hold up this much for you would he die for you or better yet are you going to die today for him." Uncle said mean every word.

"He been with some nigga putting in work lately this I know for sure but what or who they been moving on I don't know at all and I definitely don't know for sure who he been with I never seen or heard about him if I knew I would tell y'all I swear." Ty Black said.

With tears running down his face Ty Black looked Uncle in the eyes and said "but I think it was the boy G-money from up on Hawthorne Ave and Clinton Place Since I been home that's only nigga I heard Rock say anything about to my knowledge.

"Okay Ty you did a good job I actually believe you this time, aight Night kill this nigga" Uncle said. (Laugh, laugh)

"Please, please don't kill me I won't tell anyone anything just don't kill me you said I had a chance if I told you everything I knew" Ty Black said to Uncle crying.

"Naw Night he good Uncle said still laughing" the look on Ty's face was like he had just shitted on himself he was so relieved by Uncle's words.

"Come on we out y'all we got the information we came for just set this spot on fire and oh yeah Ty you do I have a chance I'm a man of my word, we out of this bitch but you alive so you better figure out a way out of here before this shit on fire like back draft my man I wouldn't want to die from being set on fire alive so good

bye my guy" Uncle said striking a match and tossing it on the gas soaked building.

"I would say you got about 15 minutes. Good Night"

Chapter 12

2 weeks later…………..

The streets had been ringing louder than the Philadelphia Liberty bell and it was clear since the kidnapping of Ty Black, Uncle was the King nobody ever saw Ty Black again. Uncle and Night didn't even know if Ty made it out of the basement that day it's not like they cared though, Uncle called his young boy Milly and told him that he wanted G-money touched he put $10,000 on his head but he wanted him brought to him alive.

The streets were buzzing everybody in the city was trying to cash in the ticket on G-money but he had been a ghost like Styles P. Nobody saw or heard from him in weeks there were a few calls people saying they saw him but he was still a ghost, G-money was becoming like Tupac and Elvis everybody was seeing a lookalike G-money.

Uncle, Ray, Night, Milly and Lockout had been bleeding the block all it was about right now was get money, pick-up and drop-off work. They were all swinging through Hawthorne Ave G-money's block and by his house on Wilcox Ave they were even beating up his mother's house in Orange, N.J.

Ray pulled up to Uncle's house in Union, N.J. Called Uncle "Yo I'm downstairs" Ray said.

"Aight I'm coming out right now" Uncle said.

It was time to go on the hunt again they wouldn't stop until they found G-money one way or another. As Uncle was getting into the car with Ray, Ray's phone went off (Ring, Ring) "Hello what's good? Ma"

It was Crystal calling she yelled to her nephew "get to the hospital Mela just woke up, I'm about to call Rah and let him know."

"He right here Ma we on our way" Ray responded.

"Okay good make sure you bring Clever" Crystal said.

"That was Crystal she said Mela woke up, she wants us to get up there and bring Clever" Ray said.

"Damn that's great go to my house lets go get Clever, wait right here" Uncle said running into the house. Gina what's up love, Mela woke up I'm taking Clever to the hospital. I want you to follow us and bring the boys, Clever come on your mother awoke and she wants to see you."

Clever came running into the living room excited it felt like Allah had giving him the greatest gift in the world "Yeah Allah answered all my prayers" Clever screamed.

Uncle and Clever went outside jumped in Ray's rental car and pulled off headed for the city.

"Hey, baby glad to see you back from the dead" Crystal said to Mela her first born child "Girl you had us all scared shitless we didn't know what was going on we thought you might not pull through at one time but you are here I love you, baby."

Tonya, Jahmela, Nicki all burst into the room, Nicki Ghetto ass started singing R-Kelly's hit song (The Storm is Over) "Damn girl you had one more day to come back to us or I was gone to kill you myself" Tonya said. Jahmela just went over and hugged her sister and kissed her on her cheeks.

Mela asked her mother "Where is Clever, is he ok?"

"Yes baby he is perfectly fine he made it out of the house that night right now he is with Ray and Rah I called them when you woke up and they are on their way here now" Crystal informed her daughter.

Kamela's next question everyone knew was coming but nobody truly knew who to answer it "Where is Haz, what room is he in is he ok? Ma"

With tears in her eyes, Crystal Kamela's mother answered her question and told her the bad news, "baby Haz didn't make it he died the night your two were shot. He was shot in the head point black range then your house was set on fire. They had his funeral 4 days ago they waited as long as they could to see if you would come out of your

coma before they had his service."

They talked another 15-20 minutes before Clever came running into the room yelling "Mommy, Mommy yeah Mommy you awake."

"Hey, baby I love you" Mela said to Clever with tears running down her cheeks.

"Mommy why are you crying you aren't happy to see everyone."

"Yes baby I glad you are all here Mommy is crying because I am so happy to see you again, I love you more than life itself." Mela said.

"I'm glad we have you back Mommy, plus grandma, Aunty, Uncle and everybody else are here I love every one of you" Clever said still crying.

"Where is Uncle at anyway?" Mela asked and if as on cue Uncle and Ray walked into the room.

"Hey cuzzo" Ray said to Mela smiling from ear to ear.

"Come on guys we have to go the Doctor's said she needs her rest, visiting hours are over we can all come back tomorrow" Uncle announced to everyone in the room.

Everybody got up and gave Mela kisses and hugs, "Okay baby I will see you tomorrow" Crystal said. When the last person left the room Uncle went to the door as if he was about to leave and locked it, Ray grabbed a seat.

"Mela we need to talk to you if you remember anything let his know, we don't have any time to waste sis shit been crazy out here while you been sleeping" with that Uncle and Ray pulled up chairs and sat next to Mela ready to hear anything she had to say.

"Mela I know it hurts right now but we need to find out who did this to you and my brother, so I need you to tell us any and everything you can remember" Uncle said.

"Okay Rah" Mela said to them (then she went back to the night she never wanted to remember, her and Haz had went out to eat. She couldn't remember where they had went but they dropped Clever off at Jahmela's, No, No she picked Clever up from school they went out to eat around 8pm. It was a celebration they were opening up a new beauty salon they talked about business and some other things. Mela had been distracted because she had been getting a lot of strange calls all day long; she decided to tell Haz about it at the dinner she knew he would be upset she hadn't told him in the beginning.

"Haz wasn't mad he said don't worry bae, I will figure out who it is I was glad he would handle everything he was a boss like that.

After we finished our dinner we danced and enjoyed the rest of the night before we went home, we picked Clever up and went home around 10pm. Clever went straight to bed Haz tucked him in and came back into the room with me, I surprised him with a police ladies outfit on."

"Haz got into bed and we made love for a next hour next thing I knew Haz was out like a light, I got up checked on Clever he was sleep too so I went back in the room got in bed and finally fell asleep myself. I woke up to two masked gunmen smacking me and shouting where is the money and drugs to Haz. Haz told the dudes the money is under the dog house just take it I don't have any drugs here."

"The gunman said if it is there then we would both live to tell the story, he told the other one, go get the money. They tied us up once we were they asked Haz where is the dog, Haz told them the dog is in the dog house then the gunman that tied us up said to the other one yo G something what do I do with the dog, the other gunman he called G something said nigga I don't give a fuck kill the shit. I can't remember his name I just know its G something."

She stopped to breath tears were pouring down her face as she continued her story.

"When he came back me and Haz where tied to the chairs, he came back with the money and told the other gunman. Yeah I found the money it was right were he said it would be they started to leave but then they stopped the gunman with the money came back and shot me then he shot Haz. I passed out after that when I finally woke up and came to I could smell smoke, and I could feel the heat I knew the house had to be on fire I tried to go to Haz but I was still tied up.

"I was bleeding bad as I struggled to get free from the ropes I finally was able to get loose I went over to check on Haz he was bleeding bad but he was still breathing so I went to Clever's room but he was gone, I went looking for him in the house but the fire and smoke were to strong and it over took me, I tried to get out of the house but I never made it." Mela took a deep breath and was finished with the story of that night.

Uncle pulled out his phone and called Night "It was definitely that nigga bruh, Mela woke up and just confirmed everything we been finding out put more pressure on the streets his family everybody bruh we gotta find this nigga now. Make it $20,000 on that boy" Uncle said then hung up just as quickly not waiting for Night to respond.

"Alright Mela we about to be out the dude you heard name G something was a guy named G-money from Hawthorne Ave we been looking for him but right now he hiding out but you just gave us the confirmation we needed, so now we going to put the full

court press on the streets. When he show up it is time to talk to the boy" Uncle said laughing knowing damn well talking was the last thing on his mind.

"Love you cousin see your tomorrow" Ray said hugging her.

"Love you two fools, be safe out there" Mela said.

Chapter 13

(I make it rain, I make it rain, I make it rain on these hoes)

G-Money sung out loud along to Lil Wayne and Fat Joe's

Anthem as he was sitting in New York City traffic, he had come home

the day before after a 2 week vacation in the Dominican Republic. He

was glad to be back on US soil he and his wife enjoyed there selves but

it was nothing like home plus his wife sure as hell knew how to spend

his money like it was going out of style, he didn't care she was his wife

but it was time to get back home to make that money back.

He had quit hustling, robbing had become too easy and he was

headed back to Jersey after meeting his boy AR from uptown, AR put

G-money on a lick for like 30-50 bandz. He had a young boy out in

Newark getting bricks from him, but the boy seemed fishy so he

decided to just rob him.

The plan was for G-Money to come out to NYC meet AR and

then follow AR's man back to Newark rob him when the opportunity

presented itself, G-Money was cool with that move.

Lockout was riding solo listening to music thinking about the moves he had been making by himself, lately with everybody focused on G-money he still needed to eat so he had been fucking with his man people out in Harlem, the work was okay nothing to write home about but the prices were too good to turn down. Lockout spotted the all-white S550 Benz following him in the city; he would wait until he got back to Jersey just to make sure he wasn't tripping. It could be the Feds, stick-up kids or nothing at all.

As he came through the Holland Tunnel he spotted the Benz once again this time much clearer, he noticed there was a black dude with dreads in the car by himself. Lockout figured it had to be a jack boy because the Feds traveled in a team, so he decided to make his move before getting on the Pulaski Skyway Bridge he put his left blinker on as if he was pulling in the left lane to go to the gas station. As soon as he got into the left lane he slammed on his brakes not giving the Benz anytime to get behind him.

Lockout's passenger window came down as G-Money's Benz pulled up alongside him (Bang, Bang, Bang, Bang, Bang) Lockout sent shots into the Benz as it got next to him then pulled off into traffic speeding back towards Newark.

G-Money was hit twice in the chest everything happened so fast he couldn't do shit but take the shots, as he went to shoot back the last bullet hit the gun and knocked it out of his hand. He pulled off headed to his home girl Tesha's house, she was a Registered Nurse she would be able to help him because a hospital wasn't an option.

He knew Uncle had money on his head and wasn't about to let a nigga cash out on him plus he couldn't risk the police being at the hospital. (Ring, Ring) "Tesha this G-Money I just got shot I need your help, I'm on my way to your house shit G-Money said when he saw the state troopers jump behind him and cut there lights on" now he had a real problem he was shot and the police but fuck going to jail he thought speeding off he jumped on the Pulaski Skyway doing a 100 mph in and out of traffic.

He had put distance between himself and the state troopers, as he got on 78 west he saw 3 more cop cars appear he was bleeding more now as his adrenaline pumped he still had a nice stretch on them but as he tried to cut right across traffic another car came out of nowhere and forced him which caused him to fish tail and hit a guard rail. He tried to get out of the car, he struggled for a while but couldn't get out then darkness set in.

When he finally woke up he was handcuffed to a hospital bed looking at 3 officers in his hospital room, Officer Sanchez read him his right as soon as he came to "You have the right to remain silent anything you do or say can and will be used against you in the court of law. You have the right to an attorney if you cannot afford one, one will be appointed to you." At this time G-Money had the look of a mad, sad and defeated man.

"You are being charged with Assault, Flee & Eluding, Possession of a weapon, Unlawful possession of a weapon, discharging a firearm and maybe there will be a few more charges to follow."

G-Money was sick but there wasn't anything he could do right now, it is what it is he still had money put up for a lawyer and bail so fuck it at least he could fight the charges he thought but he needed a call.

"Officer what's going on man I need to call my lawyer" G-Money asked.

"Sir, you are under arrest and lockdown you will not be allowed to make a call until you are released from the hospital and are down at the county jail." Officer Sanchez inform G-Money

"Yo, son I was coming back from New York, I peeped a nigga in a white S550 following me but I didn't really pay it any attention until I saw the shit again still following me once I got back to Jersey. I had to get on my movie shit son word up I hit the nigga like 5 times through his window, I think it was the nigga G-Money but I don't know for sure and I sure hell wasn't waiting around to find out" Lockout told Milly as he got inside the trap spot.

"Word son that shit sound crazy, sit the fuck down let's see if we can make some calls see what's good? But what the fuck was you doing coming from New York anyway" Milly asked knowing something was funny about the shit with Lockout.

Chapter 14

"Rah turn to the news" Mela told Uncle.

Today's weather forecast will be 75 degrees and sunny, "Breaking News currently in progress this is A.J. Ross ABC News there is currently a high speed police pursuit on 78 west of a white s550 Mercedes Benz. Reports are coming in that the pursuit started by the Holland Tunnel on the Jersey side with reports of shots being fired and as police were arriving on the scene; the white Mercedes was seen speeding off. Police then activated there lights in an attempt to stop the vehicle but the Benz speed away and the pursuit begun, Helicopters are following live in on the chase let's have a live look-in."

"Oh shit, Mela you see this wow niggas out here making movies, hope he get away though." (The car was just clipped by police in any attempted pit maneuver to try and end the chase, the driver lost control and the car slammed into the guardrail as the Helicopter cameras panned in closer)

"Damn that's the nigga G-Money I think Mela he one of the dudes that shot you, I hope he ain't dead yet." Uncle told her.

3 Days Later.................................

"Let me get 3 clips" the older black fiend said to Milly, Milly didn't usually deal with selling hand to hand to fiends but this fiend had been good money the past few months coming to cop 8 balls, ounces he was good bread.

"Aight here" Milly gave him the clips he passed Milly $300 "Aight Unk see you later"

"Aight young boy be safe, I'm see you later.

(Click, Click, Click) The fiend had been busted by Newark PD 6 months earlier and was now working with them around Newark to do buy and bust at various spots ran by Uncle and Haz. (Click, Click, Click as the undercover officers took more pictures)

Newark Police had been slowly building their case over the past 6 months Confidential Informants, buy and bust deals as time had started to past they saw Haz was the head, Uncle was next up, followed by enforcers, stash house bosses, runners and block hustlers. They ran a good operation you never saw Haz or Uncle do anything, shit they didn't even know who the stash house bosses where until Haz was killed and things started to crumble.

They streets had begun to dry up when they sent there C.I at Milly and he was able to start making purchases now here they were 6 months later they were ready to hit a couple of the stash houses and make arrest.

The C.I (Confidential Informant) exited Milly's car and left, Milly pulled off. Once he got back to the stash house they planned to hit while he was there.

Milly Pulled up to New York's Chicken shack on Clinton Ave & Seymour Ave (They had the best chicken in the city) Milly jumped out of his BMW 645 coupe ran into the chicken shack to place his order, as always hustlers and females where inside.

"What's good? Milly a couple of dudes spoke.

"Shit bruh you already know let me get some bally I need a 8th" Milly said to one of the dudes, and then he ordered his food "Let me get 2 breast, a Snapple Apple and 2 Vanilla Dutch's. 10 minutes later Milly was jumping back behind the wheel of his 645 and pulling off headed to his stash house where lockout was at to meet him.

Milly put his key in the door and opened the stash spot he threw lockout the bally when he saw him sitting at the table "Roll up nigga make yourself useful."

"Sargent do you want to hit them now Milly just got here and went inside" the undercover officer said.

"No, not yet officer stand down let them get comfortable let's try to catch them with their hands in the cookie jar, lol or with the work on the table" said Sargent Crawford.

"Here the Officer" said to G-Money throwing him some clothes "Put these on" unlocking one arm handcuff "the Doctors cleared you so you are about to get transferred down to Green Street it's time to go to jail."

(Bang, Bang, Bang, Bang) "What the fuck Lockout" said dropping the weed, Milly ran to the window it's the boys bruh (Police). **"Damn nigga where the work at" Milly asked Lockout.**

"I passed all the shit out to the runners already we good on that note in here, but I got that bread upstairs $160,000." Lockout went upstairs opened the safe took the money out of the wall safe and moved it to the floor boards put the money in here bruh, just as he did that the door came crashing down. Officers emerged from everywhere entering the apartment with guns drawn.

"Don't fucking move put your hands up, where your boys at clear" Officers upstairs yelled out "Get down we have another one" they said bringing Lockout downstairs. "We caught this one trying to jump out the window."

They cuffed both Lockout and Milly "tear this shit up I want everything, drugs, money, guns whatever in here I want" Sargent Crawford told his officers.

Officers came back 15 minutes later "Sarge, we searched everything we found a safe upstairs can't get it open, we gone have to get a locksmith up here but other than that it is clear no drugs, money, just a couple of handguns" Officer Riley said.

"Okay we can charge this one with the guns" Sargent Crawford said pointing at Lockout "we have enough on Mr. Milly send them downtown we need to talk to them.

Ring, Ring, Ring) "Hello, who this" Uncle asked picking up his phone.

"Uncle, this Ju from Seymour Ave the boys just ran into Milly and Lockout spot, they hit the stash house about a hour ago locked both them niggas up."

"Aight good look Ju let me see what the fuck going on out here" Uncle said hanging up.

(Ring, Ring) "Jahmela, they just hit one of my spots" Uncle said.

"Hold on, Hold on hello Rah" Jahmela said stopping Rah mid-sentence.

"Oh sorry miss lady, hey Jah I need a big favor they hit one of my spots grabbed up a few of my men. I need help finding

86

them and any information you can give me about G-Money would be helpful also bae" Uncle said before he even realized it, Jahmela was caught off guard but tried to act normal.

"Okay, Rah I will see what I can find out I will call you back when I know something and remember you surely do owe me" Jah said.

"Separate these two put them in rooms for questioning, no lawyers nothing yet just let them sit in the rooms until I'm ready to talk" Sargent Crawford said to his commanding officer Riley.

Milly sat in the room cuffed to the table, his mind was wondering what they had and what the charges would be but he knew this was about Uncle and Haz. He and Lockout weren't that big in the game yet but he wasn't know snitch, some niggas would tell on niggas and still went down (prison) or came home like they ain't do shit wrong, fuck that he had death b4 dishonor tatted on his arm and he would stand by that, he was sure Lockout would stand tall also.

Sargent Crawford walked into the room where Lockout was at first he figured Lockout would break first "How is it going today Mr. Kennedy, I'm Sargent Crawford I would like to offer you an olive branch a chance to help yourself, help me help you. I know you work for Rashaan Anderson AKA Uncle. We don't want you or your boy Milly we want him not y'all. (Lockout interrupted)

"I ain't got shit to say to you or nobody else I want my lawyer that's it that's all" with that being said Sargent Crawford got up and said "Okay suit yourself but let's see if your boy going to hold up as strong as you" and got up and left the room.

Next up was Milly, Sarge realized he would have to change strategies because his tactics with Lockout didn't work at all plus he knew Milly was raised under Uncle and would be a lot harder to break if at all.

"Riley go get Detective Smith up here, I want him to question this perp" (Smith was a street smart young black Detective he would relate to Milly better he was the best chance they had.) Smith showed up 5 minutes later "how can I help Sarge" Detective Smith asked.

Smith I need you go in there and talk to this suspect named Melvin Mills AKA Milly, we have him in on numerous drug, and weapons charges but what we really want is information on his boss Rashaan Anderson AKA Uncle" Sarge told Smith briefing him.

"Okay Sarge I'm ready, send me in."

"What's good my boy, Million dollar Milly is it what it do I'm Detective Smith. I'm going to keep it 100 with you my nigga they got you and your man, we got a C.I. you been serving the past

6 months, we grabbed guns out the apartment I'm sure they probably got bodies on them, got gun in your car, you looking at a least 25 to life but I'm willing to make everything go away. We want Uncle not you or your boy over there, Uncle is the man plus your man Lockout already switched sides I suggest you do the same we just need some confirmation on things he told us."

"Fuck you nigga this my shit I'm the boss around here I don't know no fucking Lockout so whatever he said some bullshit, bitch ass nigga just take me to jail cause I don't know shit" Milly yelled.

"Aight fuck it player we got Lockout he can tell on you to and them you dumb fuck" said Detective Smith

Jahmela called Rah back "They are downtown being questioned" she told Uncle.

"Okay Thank You, Jah" Uncle responded.

"You are welcome Rah but you know you owe me dinner and a movie nigga" Jahmela told him.

"Okay babe you got it and a lot more love bae" Rah said.

Rosenberg showed up 20 minutes later making all kinds of threats and promises, but it worked somewhat he got Lockout and Milly both bails. The case against Milly was strong damn near airtight but Lockout was just basically caught at the wrong place at the wrong time; they had nothing on him so he was good. Uncle bailed Milly and Lockout both out but Milly wasn't being released because he had a warrant for a VOP (Violation of Probation) but Lockout was supposed to get released sometime today.

Chapter 15

1 Month Later………………..

In the short time since the murder of his father and the attempted murder of his mother Clever had grown-up more than his years and was becoming a very smart and cunning young man. He was still staying with Uncle while his mother was in the Rehabilitation Center, he and his cousins were getting closer everyday Tah was his best friend and Aunt Gina was becoming his second mother.

Uncle was always gone it was like he didn't even stay there anymore but when he did come around Clever would notice the stressed out look in his eyes.

Clever's birthday was coming up in a few days and he was excited to be turning 11 years old.

"Aye Auntie Gina can you please take me to see my mother" Clever asked.

"Yes baby no problem just give me a few minutes to get ready" Gina responded.

The boys had went to Gina's mother's house so this would give her some free time once she dropped Clever off at the hospital, he was a great kid quick to learn anything you taught him and do before ever thing happened. Now he was coming out of his shell more acting up sometimes but that was to be expected knowing what he went through she just hoped he would be okay.

"Come on Clever lets go" Gina said grabbing her keys and heading out of the front door. Gina pulled up in front of the Rehab Center on Jay Street in Newark, double parked and took Clever inside.

"Hello miss, how can I help you today?" the Receptionist asked Gina.

"Yes Hi, I'm here to bring my nephew to see his mother Kamela Anderson, I'm her sister-in-law Gina Anderson."

"Okay Mrs. Anderson, Kamela is in room 204 you have to get on the elevator right down the hall there and get off on the second floor, make a left when you get off the elevator" the receptionist informed Gina.

Gina made sure Clever found his way up to his mother's room said hi to Kamela and left to enjoy her free day. "Bye Clever see you later"

Kamela was looking much better these days "Hey mommy".

"Come here little man give your mother a hug and kiss"
she tried to kiss him.

Clever and his mother talked for a while, Clever made his mother feel better every time he came to see her almost made her forget that horrible life changing night when she almost died and lost the love of her life, but as soon as she was alone again. Everything in her mind would go back to that night everything would just come flooding back like it was on a permanent replay in her mind.

"I love you mommy, I want to take care of you forever and ever when you get older just like daddy you will always have me. I'm going to be a cop so I can lock up the people who did this to you and daddy." Clever told his mother

"Okay baby you can be anything you want to be a Doctor,
a Lawyer, a Cop or anything else in this world. I can't wait for you
to get big and take care of me but you are already taking care of
me little man." Kamela told her son.

"Mommy why did Allah let this happen to our family, was I bad or daddy or something I'm sorry mommy when are we going home, I love Uncle house but I'm ready to go home" Clever told his mother.

"Me too little man, I'm more than ready to go home and no you didn't do anything wrong Allah always has a plan he loves us but there are bad people in this world" Kamela told he son.

"Okay mommy I hope Allah gets all the bad people in the world especially the people that did this to you and daddy" Clever said hugging his mother.

The Doctor entered the room "Hello, Mrs. Anderson how are you feeling today. What's going on little guy how's mommy feeling? "

"I'm great Doc feeling like I'm ready to go home now." Kamela said.

"Well today is your luck day I guess, we have a few more standard test we need to perform and if everything comes back good you will be discharged today" the Doctor told Kamela.

Chapter 16

6 months later..........

"Shit has been crazy the past 6 months bruh I been living with my head on a swivel I know them people coming one of these days, I ain't gone lie shit got me shook" Uncle said to Night.

"Yeah bruh I already know I been seeing all kinds of suspect shit, I'm here for your forever I love you my nigga. Night said meaning every last word he had just spoken.

"What's good with the boy Milly how he holding up, you think he on some ratting shit or what? Because you already know jail can't save him from a good night if he on some bullshit" Night said.

"Naw my young boy a stand up nigga he good, he took his time like a man never said a word he get sentenced tomorrow he copped out to a 6 with a 42" (6years with mandatory 42 months). **Shit definitely been real thou when he first got bagged and got to the county he called me through his lawyer.**

(Ring, Ring) "Hello, what you want Rosenberg, what you need more money" Uncle asked when he picked up thinking it was all his lawyers ever wanted.

"No Mr. Anderson I got Milly on the line" Rosenberg responded

"What's good big bruh, good looking for the lawyer but I called with a gift for you, the nigga G-money just came in my cell earlier we still in quarantine, so he ain't gone be my Bunkie long but I want to know if you want me to just hit the nigga now I know you wanted him alive before" Milly asked.

"Not now young bull, just watch the nigga get to know him be his boy get as close to him as you can see if he give up some information about the robbery. But don't ask him about it just see if he let it slip out, until then let him live" Uncle said to Milly. Uncle didn't want to make shit worse on his boy right now, everything would come to light in due time.

"Aight big bruh be safe out there the pigs want you bad stay 10 toes, I fell don't do the same the world need you out there." Milly, told Uncle before hanging up the phone.

"Good, I like that little nigga ain't want to have to be the cause of his demise" Night said to Uncle.

"Where the fuck this nigga Lockout at, I told him be here at 12pm, we all need to talk" Uncle said he and Night where at the day bar Chester's on Broadway in North Newark aka Spanish Harlem.

"I don't know ever since you stepped away from the frontline and let him drive the car the nigga on some big headed shit always late, probably was with some bitch all night or some shit. If it wasn't because of you I wouldn't be fucking with the nigga no more but I know somebody gotta watch him before he bring us all down" Night said.

"Yeah I already know, I still got eyes and ears everywhere on these streets but right now shit far more destructive than I thought it's not just Newark Police on us any more, we got the Federal Government everywhere now as we speak they outside my house, and the beauty salon." Uncle said.

"Last week I got pulled over on High and Spruce Street (Dr. Martin Luther King Blvd) cops got out there cars in suits and shit walked up to my car like hello Mr. Anderson or better yet the infamous Uncle how's your day. Get this these pigs passed me a card and said I should help myself because my days are numbered, they went back to their cars jumped in and pulled off" Uncle Said.

"Here the nigga go right here" Night said seeing Lockout come through the door.

"Lock it 12:30 nigga I know I asked you to be here at 12 what's good bruh" Uncle asked Lockout.

"My bad Uncle, my BM (baby mother) started tripping earlier talking a bunch of other shit, I had to handle that before the bitch tried to shoot me or some shit. But what's good big bruh" Lockout said to them lying through his teeth.

"Aight look peep this I got the feds coming for me so I can't make no more moves, I can't even be seen with none or y'all anymore. I know they probably watching y'all too but right now they only on me, most likely they think Lockout you just a small time worker, so from here on out I'm becoming a ghost out of sight out of mind. I'm giving you and Night the connect; Lock some of the prices I was getting you and Night will get but here's the thing he doesn't want to do any direct business with either of you right now.

Y'all are too close to the Federal investigation on me, so I'm bringing in a new dude in the fold he family Night you already know Ray and Lockout I Vouch for him and so can Night." Uncle said to both his soldiers.

(Uncle had been doing business with Ray since the murder of Haz, once Mela woke up Ray stayed up north about a month then decided to go back to the ATL were he had his peoples, he was making trips once a month getting birds from Uncle and flying them down south, plus Uncle trusted him not that he didn't trust Night or Lockout but Night was a shooter not a real hustler and Lockout was young, you couldn't give these new age young niggas everything they would cross you like Broad and Market Street.)

"So here's how everything will work from here on out until further notice, Ray will get the shipments from the connect handle all the money you give him for the payment to the connect. Lockout you will still be the front man Alpha Dog nothing on your end changes you still will handle all the work after Ray passes off to you, stash houses and runners become you and Night's responsibility not just yours anymore Night. Ray reports to both of you if any problems arise Night you call my lawyer those are the only calls I'm going to take from you two."

"Night you know Ray and most likely y'all going to have to put in work together, so I want you to keep a close eye on him when he is up here he still will be back and forth from here and Atlanta. I need both of y'all on your A games, I need you to be my eyes and ears. Are y'all both cool with this new setup, if you got any objections let me know now before we leave this table" Uncle said finish telling everybody the new business proposal he set forth.

"I'm good with it Rah, I just enjoying the ride ready to get back to this money bruh" Night said

"What about you" Uncle said looking Lockout in the eyes, he knew Lockout would have a problem not being the one to go straight to the connect because shit if it was him he would have a problem with it. Lockout eyes said he had a problem but Uncle wanted to see if Lockout would admit it to them.

"I ain't going to lie big homie, I'm salty the connect won't fuck with me or Night but if you trust Ray then I'm with you plus me and Night going to be watching him. I just got one question who the fuck is he and where he at?" Lockout said

"I'm right here" Ray said walking up he had been sitting close by listening, Uncle wanted him to hear Lockout so he could get a feel for him before they met.

"I'm family we all family and in my family we practice loyalty, smarts and always death before dishonor. I'm ready to make this money bruh, Rah under the Federal eye which means you two are too so we all move accordingly no sloppy shit if they gone come then they leave how they came and that is guessing, we got to keep them guessing." Ray said.

"Alright gentlemen if we all on the same page then I'm out, Night I need you to come with me got a few moves I need to

make and I going to need your help before I get low. You two Uncle said to Lockout and Ray can stay here get to know each other, we about to be out 1 love" Uncle said dapping them both.

Night got up said "see y'all later" and followed Uncle out of the bar. When Night and Uncle got in the car and pulled off Night asked "so what you got to do Rah."

"Naw I'm good bruh I just wanted them niggas to chill together a minute before we all jumped straight to doing business together, plus I wanted to tell you to watch Lockout and Ray we both know him but still make sure they good, we can't let these nigga be our downfall Night" Uncle said.

"I'm going to drop you back off to your car and I'm a be out need to do something special for the wife today" Uncle said

"He just dropped Night off at Chester's Bar we are in position to take him down boss" said the FBI agent following Uncle into his walkie talkie.

"No wait just continue to follow him I will let you know when to move, wait for back-up" FBI agent in charge Wilson said back into his walkie talkie.

Uncle dropped Night off back to his car and headed to Short Hills Mall, we wanted to surprise her with something tonight at dinner.

He saw the car following him he knew it was the Feds he called his lawyer told him be on stand by and hoped he would make it to his Dinner date tonight with his wife.

Uncle got to the mall picked out a Diamond Necklace and Tennis Bracelet to match brought a few other things and headed out of the mall and back to his car, what he saw when he made it to his car broke his heart not because he was about to go to jail he was ready for that but because he couldn't have this night with his wife. He knew they both needed it but it would not be happening.

Rashaan Anderson the white FBI agent said stopping Uncle as he tried to get in his car, you are under arrest you have the right to remain silent. The officer read him the rest of his right.

Uncle dropped his bag and let the officer place his handcuffs on his wrist, today would not be the day another black man got shot down by the police. He would fight this fight in the court room.

Chapter 17

2 ½ years later.........................

Time was flying by Clever was turning 14 years old soon
and becoming a very handsome and smart young man, he was living
with his mother now but rarely ever home these days. Between his
mother's boyfriend and his new girlfriend home was the last place he
wanted to be, plus he had more freedom and fun at Aunt Gina's house
with his cousins.

Since Uncle had gotten arrested Gina was all over the place
mentally she wasn't anything close to herself, Clever truly thought that
maybe she was getting high he knew she was stressing bad but she had
lost a lot of weight.

His cousins could careless Lil Rah was 13 years old and
feeling nothing but girls, Tah was 12 years old and was already on the
path to take over his father's place in the streets, he already had a crew
of young home boys who followed him around doing whatever he told
them to do. (Uncle would call and talk to them but what could he really

say or do he still had at least 7 more years to do before he even had a chance to come home.)

The day at the mall Uncle had been arrested on multiple drug and kingpin charges, he fought the charges as long as he could but they had him and his lawyer advised him his best option was to take the deal the Feds had to offer. The Federal government had a 98% conviction rate and if he went to trial he would definitely lose.

Uncle knew that the Feds would want him to snitch but he wasn't going out like that so if he did take a deal his lawyer would have to figure something out because he wasn't telling shit. His lawyer came up with the idea to basically if they wanted information Rah would just blame everything on his dead brother, so he decide to take the deal 15 years with 85% to do behind bars.

Clever did the best that he could do to help his cousins but he was still growing up himself, he had his first real girlfriend now, she was a cute black and Korean girl from Union, N.J. She was a year older than him and was real bossy her name was Leah.

He didn't know what real love was but he definitely was in lust with her they would go to the movies, the skating rink they hadn't had sex yet she wasn't ready so Clever didn't push her, he still was a virgin himself.

"Clever, Clever hello anybody home" Lil Rah said snapping him out of his day dream. "Damn cuzzo where was your brain at you sitting over there looking at the fucking stars and shit here hit the bally."

"My bad Lil Rah, I was in fantasy land thinking about Leah and shit I'm ready to hit that shit bruh but she acting like she scared" Clever said.

"I don't know what to tell you big cuzzo you could always do like me and get you a new bitch my nigga, shit you already know I got a couple for you ready but they all scared of Leah so they don't be trying to say shit to you." Lil Rah told Clever.

"Naw Lil cuzzo I'm good, where the fuck your brother at I barely ever see his little ass anymore" Clever said.

"I don't even know Clever that nigga think he a thug, he always rolling with his clown ass homies them niggas all some punks. Pops told me to try to slow him down on some big brother shit but pops been gone he don't know how Tah out here coming."

"We do and you know that little nigga out here thinking he grown so I'm going to let him do him, we up here in Union he ain't seen the real streets yet, matter of fact Clever let's all take a trip down to the hood go to Avon Ave in Newark show him what's really good cause he is really out here bugging." Lil Rah said

"Alright I'm cool with that I'm going to call Night tomorrow" Clever told Lil Rah. **"I'm out my mom want me to come home tonight, peace cuzzo."**

(Clever got home about 30 minutes later.)

"What's going on Ma? Why you sitting her in the dark, what is the matter that nigga Devin ain't put his hands on you." Clever asked.

"No baby that's not it he wouldn't ever do that, nor would I ever allow that" Mela told her son.

"So why are you sitting here in the dark crying, Ma" Clever asked.

"He asked me to marry him earlier, I had to tell him I wasn't ready for that kind of commitment he got upset and left me at the restaurant, and when I came home I pulled out these old pictures the first one I came across was of me and your father's wedding. That is why I'm sitting here crying."

"I called you to come home because I knew you would stay out at Gina's house and I want to go through these pictures with you and get your advice on somethings. Do you think I should marry Devin, you know you have to walk me down the aisle so if you don't approve I can't marry him." Mela said

"Ma I love you so, even though I don't really like Devin I know he a good dude he don't like me either but he make you happy and treat you good. So if you love him you can go ahead and accept his proposal I can't wait to walk you down the aisle." Clever said **"Now let's look at these pictures."**

"Thank you baby I'm going to call him later and talk to him, I hope he still wants to marry me." Mela told Clever. (Looking at the pictures Mela felt good) "Clever how is your girlfriend, I like her are y'all still together."

"Yeah Ma she still rolling with me you know I'm a fly boy she can't resist me" Clever said.

"Okay, Mr. Irresistible I know you better be using condoms because I'm not ready to be a grandmother boy. You still have to go to college" Kamela told her first and only child.

"Oh yeah and tell your bad ass little cousin he better calm his ass down, Gina might be losing her mind she may even be getting high maybe she won't do anything about him but I will come over there and fuck Tah little ass up matter of fact I'm going to call Night he can go over there and handle things" Mela said.

Chapter 18

"What's good? My boy what happened did you get that date my nigga" G-money asked Milly when he entered their cell.

Milly and G-Money had both been down (GSYF) Garden State Youth Faculty the past 18 months, Uncle had Jahmela pull a few power moves to get them both transferred into the same cell together once he found out they were both down, Yardville. They had been Bunkie's 13 months since the last time they were in the county in quarantine together and had become somewhat friends they both talked about the life they lived on the streets the drugs, drug dealing, hustling, robberies, females and a lot more.

Milly had made sure he never mentioned Lockout or Uncle's name he was in the cell with G-Money to get information not give up information but as of yet G-Money hadn't let anything of value slip out, he never mentioned anybody that was with him on any of his jux.

Milly started smiling "yeah bruh they fuck around and let a real nigga go they give me parole I got 6 months left, my date is August 18th 2013."

"True, True I'm happy as hell for you my guy, shit I feel like I'm going home gives me something to look forward to with you, all I got is 14 months left once you leave we both get out there and get back to that bag" G-Money said.

"You already know I'm about to go out here and run it up, never let these crackers get me again that's a fact my boy anything you need I got you real nigga shit, but fuck all that right now here" Milly said throwing the package to G-Money

"Roll up nigga let's get high, I'm about to go get the phone got some calls to make don't light that shit until I get back nigga you know you be steaming the bally" Milly said getting up off his bunk headed to Re-Mo's cell.

Re-Mo was a straight up fool all the C.Os were scared of him so Milly let him hold the cell phone down because he knew nobody was gone try and search Re-Mo's cell and he wasn't trying get caught with the phone that was an automatic 5 years flat added to your bid.

"Yo, Re-Mo what's good? Bruh let me get the jack" Milly said to Re-Mo.

"Alright, bruh hold on let me get it what happened when you went to see the parole board" Re-Mo asked before he handed Milly the phone and the charger.

109

**"Shit green my boy I got my date, I'm out in 6 months"
Milly told Re-Mo.**

"Aight my nigga stay sucker free you already know these young bulls in here ready to start hating, cause you going to be leaving and they staying so make sure you watch your back and front" said Re-Mo.

Milly dapped Re-Mo and left the cell, when he got back to his cell G-Money had 2 sticks (Rollies) of weed rolled up. Milly cut on the radio Camron's classic hit (Oh Boy) was playing Milly lit up one of the sticks and started the beat down (Conversation) with G-Money.

He only had 6 months left now he thought there was no time to waste if he was going to get the information form G-Money about the third person involved with the robbery and murder of Haz.

Passing the weed to G-Money, Milly asked "What's the wildest shit you have done for that paper."

"Shit I don't even know my boy, I done did a lot of crazy shit for that bag (money), I got to think about that one" G-Money said. "What about you, young bull."

Milly had been thinking about trying this new technique on G-Money the past week, he had come up with the idea of starting this kind of beat down and telling G-Money the hardest story of his life some of it true some of it not but if it worked he thought G-Money would be so gassed he might let the information slip out.

Milly figured he didn't have anything to lose he figured G-Money would tell him about the robbery/murder and arson of Haz unless he had some more gangster shit than that to talk about.

Giving him time to think Milly said "Like 8 years ago me and my man Red Dot (RIP) had a jux setup kidnap a plug from Washington Heights wifey, and make her call the nigga hold her for ransom."

"Damn y'all niggas were on some movie shit" G-Money said.

"Yeah word niggas was young, broke and hungry you know the shit, so peep after we snatched the bitch up we took her to a basement, tied her up we asked her to call her man and tell him we got her. We want $50,000 for you back safe and sound."

"So she called him crying telling him she got grabbed up off the street and all that but the nigga just hung up on her, so we called again this time I get on the phone. Look nigga we got your bitch I want $50,000 for her safe return, you know what the nigga said. (No)

"The Nigga said fuck that bitch kill here she costing me to much damn money anyway." *(Damn)*

"Yeah she heard him because I had him on speakerphone, she busted out crying even more like please, please don't kill me I don't want to die. My nigga Red dot was on some other shit he got mad started smacking and screaming at shorty then out of nowhere he said you kind of cute take off your clothes, I want some of that pussy and it might just save your life."

"I start thinking this nigga Red Dot crazier than a motherfucker, he fucked shorty and when he was finished he said Milly she good let her live, she rolling with us now."

"She had come up with a plan to get the money from ole boy, she was mad as hell the nigga wouldn't pay so she got down with the move. All I could say was damn that shit must be good, what the new plan is and how you know it ain't a setup."

"She looked me in my eyes and said hello my name is Christina and we all heard what he said on the phone, fuck a setup I want some payback and payment. I can't just take y'all to his apartment because we called him already now he going to be on alert but today is Thursday and he goes to El Puerto the seafood spot every Thursday, I doubt he change that.

"He only goes to get the seafood because after that he goes to pick up drugs. I guess he uses the seafood smell to mask the drugs or some shit like that he don't think I know what he doing but he always been stupid and sloppy."

"I don't know how much drugs he pick up or if he be having money after he get the drugs but we can be at the seafood spot then follow him and once he pick up the drugs you can rob him and kill him. I liked the plan but I'm like what you mean we can follow him no you going to stay here an me and Red Dot going to follow him" Milly said telling G-Money the story.

"No, no I'm going too y'all not going to come up then say fuck me, plus y'all don't know which stop he going to make that is the pick-up but I do she said. We worked out a few more details of the plan and headed to El Puerto to wait for his arrival when his black Infiniti G35 finally arrived he did exactly what she said he would do."

"He came out of the restaurant with two big bags of seafood, the crazy part was after the call earlier it looked like the boy was stupid enough to be by himself. He seemed totally careless not a care in the world we followed him to 156th street & Broadway in Manhattan he went into an apartment with one of the seafood bags and a small book bag."

"Christina said this was the first pick-up, once he came back out he had the seafood bag but not the book bag, she said sometimes he made a drop-off or another pick-up next. So we decide to keep following him his next stop was on 7th Ave & 126th Street. When he pulled up in front of the building he got out looked around grabbed one of the seafood bags."

"Christina said she didn't know what was going on now but me and Red Dot knew instantly what was going on he was about to make a sale you already know we street niggas gotta pick up on the signs. Once he checked his waist for his strap we knew 100 percent, once he went into the building we sprang into action, Christina you get in the driver's seat keep the car running, Red Dot you post up across the street from the building entrance."

"Make sure you can see who coming out the building, I'm going to stand off to the side of the building once you see him coming out the building cross the street start walking towards the building. I'm going to do the same thing, we grab the nigga up take the money he come out with, get the keys he got kill the stupid nigga and we out."

"Oh yeah guys he has a safe at his house too, since y'all going to get him here we can go to his house and hit his safe too I already know the combination Christina told us. Alright ma one thing at a time let us get him first, come on before he come out Red Dot said."

"20 minutes later the robbery went off without a hitch exactly according to the plan and we were headed to the apartment following Christina while her ex lay in a pool of blood in the middle of a NYC sidewalk. We got away with 3 and a half kilos and $33,000 damn karma a bitch I thought headed to the apartment.

"We got to his apartment in Washington Heights, me, Christina and Red Dot all went up and I can't lie his shit was lit Christina went and emptied the safe while me and Red Dot ransacked the apartment after we were finished in total we walked away with $150,000, 3 straps, a Cuban link, Rolex, and Christina not a bad days work" Milly said finally finishing his story.

"So what about you" Milly asked "I know you done did a lot of crazy shit all you do is rob and kill shit nigga."

(G-Money rolled up another stick, lit it up slowly exhaled and started talking.)

"Damn my nigga word up you crazy as shit, you talking about Red Dot that got killed down Seth Boyden in 2008 " G-Money said.

"Yeah that was bruh RIP got caught slipping but that was my nigga gets no bigger." Milly said.

"Yeah I knew bruh he was a fly nigga word just like my man Two5 always ready to get that money, I remember my man Two5 put me on a 100 bandz lick out in Montclair, N.J. shit was supposed to be

115

an B & E (Breaking and Entering). Two5 knew the nigga and said he had money stashed under his dog house, but when we got there they were home a dude and his girl so we decided to go in tie them up and get the money and see what else they had."

"We broke in the house found their room they were both in bed sleeping me and my other dude went in smacked them up, woke them up. Dude gave up the money no problem said it wasn't nothing else in the house the problem started when the stupid nigga I was with, I told him to go get the money he asked about the dog. I said nigga I don't give a fuck about no dog kill that shit if you got to go just go get the money."

"The nigga fucked up and said my name we were masked up so it was just going to be a robbery until that stupid motherfucker said my name. Once that happened we couldn't let them live no more so we ended up having to kill both of them and then we set the house on fire. After we got out of there I had to kill the stupid nigga I did the lick with if he was that dumb enough to say my name during a robbery, then he would say my name to them people if that pressure hit. You already know better to be safe than sorry" G-Money said.

"You ain't never lied about that my boy gotta talk care of them fuck niggas before they take care of you" Milly said. "Are you going to the yard today?"

"Yeah I got to go kick it with one of my bruhs he just got down here last week" G-Money said.

"Alright let me go get in this shower, I need to make a couple of calls then I'm coming out too about to go extra hard on the workout shit. Milly said (Milly would get into the shower cut the water on then use the phone because nobody could hear or see him in the shower)

His first call was Jahmela she would let Uncle know everything he had just found out from G-Money, Next he called Christina.

"What up Chrissy how you doing out there, I miss you sis can't wait to get out in that world. Guess what sis? (What Milly) **I went to see the parole board today I got my date I come home in 6 months.**

Chrissy Screamed yes bruh I can't wait to see you with your big headed ass she said laughing.

(Rec out, Rec out, last call for rec)

"Alright sis they calling out for rec I'm about to go out I'm going to call you back later, Love you."

"Okay bruh I love you too talk to you later" Chrissy responded.

Chapter 19

"Hey Mr. Lockett how has business been treating you, looking good I see" Ray stated to his new Atlanta business partner of the past few months.

They had went into business together on a strip club after a chance meeting at a local coffee shop, Mr. Lockett had been waiting on a previous business partner to show up and he was running late. That day Ray could see the anger written on his face but this wasn't his concern. He had a dude looking to buy some kilos from him in front of him talking but Ray didn't like this joker's vibe, so he just remained quiet if he was a cop or a snitch he wouldn't get him on tape saying anything incriminating.

Mr. Lockett had been in the streets along time and even though he was now mostly a legit business man, the meeting he was supposed to be having was about getting into the drug market opening up in Atlanta. He spotted the casually dressed black man across the room listening to the thugged out looking cat in front of him but it was strange the gangster looking cat looked like he was faking it.

Mr. Lockett thought they must be working on some kind of illegal shit but the casual dressed man seemed uninterested in the deal because he wasn't saying much of anything at all.

Mr. Lockett watched for another 15 minutes he was about to leave when the wannabe gangster got up and said 22.5 right extra loud the other guy just nodded his head up and down not saying a word. Hearing this Mr. Lockett knew his guess was correct and this was a drug deal, the wannabe was a buyer and a stupid one but either he was a buyer or a cop and it looked like the other guy was a connect.

The wannabe gangster left the coffee shop and Mr. Lockett decided to get up and walk over to the connects table, he had remained seated watching the other guy walk out to his car.

"Hello, sir how are you doing I'm Mr. Lockett I don't mean to be nosey but I couldn't help but notice your exchange with your friend there."

Ray looked up saw the smiling black man in front of him dressed to the 9's in an Armani Suit, Salvatore Ferregamo shoes and thought what the hell he wanted.

Before he got a chance to say another word the hood came out of Ray "what the fuck you want and why you watching me nigga."

"Naw, Naw bruh I come in peace (Noticing the up north accent Ray had Mr. Lockett felt a connection with him already) I just have a few things to say if I am right then we may be of some sort of help to one another" Mr. Lockett said.

"Okay have a seat Mr. Lockett, I am Ray how can we help each other out I am dying to find out this helpful information."

"Alright look I don't know you and you don't know me so first let me properly introduce myself I'm Kevin Lockett aka Kev, I'm from Newark, N.J. I hear your up north accent too where you from (I'm from Newark too) Damn that's crazy bruh but I knew you had to be from up top somewhere, I been down here a minute now thou."

"I have a couple of businesses my club is the newest thing I'm trying to get jumping, I also have a small record label I working on." Mr. Lockett told Ray.

"I have a guess about you and the dude that just left; I watched your exchange with him I think he is a small time hustler or cop trying to do business with you. I didn't know what role you played in this but after hearing him say 22.5 out loud before he left, I decided to approach you because that made me believe you are plugged into some part of the drug business. I figured you must be a connect or some type of liaison to one."

"I'm not trying to be all in your business but I'm in the game knee deep and I have been looking for a new connect. Down here I been thinking about opening up shop and I think you may be able to help me here's my card. If I am right give me a call, do your research whatever you have to do" Mr. Lockett said getting up and walking out of the coffee shop.

He could tell by the look Ray gave him when he said he was looking for a connect, that Ray was definitely in the game or had access but wasn't trying to show anything. Mr. Lockett knew Ray would try and figure him out find out whatever he could; it's not every day you meet a black man dressed in a suit asking about a drug connect. Plus they were both from Newark, he was pretty sure Ray would call him.

Ray had a friend in the Atlanta Police Department he had him run a check on Kevin Lockett but he never thought about to have Jahmela do the same thing on him up in Jersey.

It had been 2 and half years since Uncle was arrested that eventful day at Short Hills Mall since then he had been shipped all across the United States. He was now at the U.S.P (United States Penitentiary) in Arizona, he and Jahmela had become very close friends again. She was his strength in a bad spot; she kept him in the know about his son's, their nephew Clever and a bunch of other shit that was going on. She even tried to help Gina get clean once she found out she was using, she tried to visit him when she could a couple of times when he was in Pennsylvania.

She also got Mela to come with her, she was falling back in love with Rah and again she thought it was great but he had a lot of time to do so. She tried her best to be his friend in this time of need; she knew he still wanted revenge for Haz's murder. She had information today for him about that very thing, she knew he would feel a lot better after this visit plus his chance to get a reduced sentence was looking better every day his lawyer told her a few days earlier.

"Rashaan Anderson Visit" the C.O. told Uncle once he got to the cell door.

"Alright I'm on my way" Uncle told the C.O. getting ready for his visit.

Uncle knew Jahmela was coming he put on his visit clothes, brushed his teeth and headed to the dance floor aka the visit hall.

Uncle had a love hate relationship with the visits he would get, he loved to see Jah but wished she could bring his son's and Clever he missed his boys. But she refused to bring them she didn't want them to ever see the inside of these walls. Stepping on to the dance floor there were a lot of brothers getting hugs and kisses from loved ones, Uncle could see beautiful wives, kids, and fathers, mothers, all kind of people.

He scanned the room looking for Jahmela when he saw her, his heart melted she was 34 years old now but didn't look a day over 25, her smile was radiant she waved at him when she spotted him as he walked over towards her.

Jahmela got up, Uncle came over hugged her and kissed her on the check.

"Hey Jah what's up? Love how are you feeling how's everybody doing?" Uncle asked.

"I'm good Rah same ole same ole work and the kids, Clever growing up fast getting tall as you and Mela she ok her boyfriend proposed to her last week, your son good other than that everybody okay." Jahmela said.

"Damn I didn't even know she had a man now she getting married but if he a good dude then that's great for them, how about my sons have you saw them lately I've been calling but I never reach anybody at the house" Uncle stated.

"I saw Clever a couple of weeks ago he told me to let you know everything was good, Lil Rah be with him a lot but Tah want to be a gangster like father like son, so they are planning on take him to Newark to see Night. Don't worry about them Clever and Lil Rah good

123

kids they will be okay all they worrying about right now are girls, they will be okay. I'm trying to get Gina back in the rehab I never really liked her but she needs help and your kids need their mother" Jahmela said.

"How's your appeal looking is everything coming along good?" Jahmela asked.

"Not a good chance at an appeal really anymore but I got a chance at getting a reduced sentence, trying to get this 12 years dropped to 8 years" Uncle told Jahmela looking deep into her eyes.

"Well that's a good thing, Rah I got something to tell you as well that's why I had to come down here before my usual visit. Milly called me he doesn't call me normally so I knew it had to be something important going on when he called. He told me to tell you he went to see the parole board and they gave him a date to come home in August, he also told me to let you know he finally got the information about Haz."

"He said some nigga named G-Money got put on the robbery by some dude named Two5 and that the dude that shot Mela and killed Haz, died the same night they did the robbery something about him saying G-Money's name so he had to die. He said he didn't know who Two5 was but we both know that got to be the one and only Two5, so I checked to see if he was home yet and guess what he been home. He got released from Rahway almost 4 years ago." Jahmela finished telling Rah.

(Jahmela had just dropped a bomb on Uncle and his fuse was lit.)

"I knew he was mad back in the day when Haz left them during the fucked up robbery shit but he made the wrong choice that day he could've gotten away too, Haz made the right one by leaving. Why comeback and kill Haz" it didn't make since but **Two5 would pay one day and it would definitely be sooner rather than later.**

Ray had been waiting on the information he had researched to all come in on Mr. Lockett before he made his decision on what to do about the potential business relationship. He had been hearing a lot of good things about Kevin Lockett; he had heard he was running a small record label called Twenty Five hits. He had a local rapper named I.b. making some noise in the ATL and a couple other businesses; he was the front money man for he had a few spots in Bankhead and Decatur moving work.

If Ray's Atlanta police contact gave him the all clear he thought he might give Kevin Lockett a call and setup a meeting to get to know him a little bit better.

(Ring, Ring, Ring Hello)

"Yeah Ray this Mr. Lockett guy is everything you think he is, he is a stand up dude from Newark, N.J. He has a record in Jersey did time up there for robbery, attempted murder and some other shit, he has been clean since he got out of prison. He's a small time business man with his hands still in the street level businesses as well, he isn't under investigation by the Atlanta Police Department as of yet so in my opinion you can open up a club with him, if you choose to."

"Okay thank you Dan good looking on that I got that for you whenever you come see me" Ray said hanging up the phone he was glad he got some good information on Mr. Lockett.

(Ring, Ring)

"Hello, this is Ray I would like to have a sit down with you and talk we can discuss a few things this Friday at Magic City 10:00pm good for you."

"Yeah main man it works for me, see you there" Mr. Lockett said in response to Ray's call.

Uncle sat in his cell the night Jahmela left and was a little bit lost at the moment, he sat in a deep reverie thinking about his life and how he got to this point. His family was in shambles almost completely

126

destroyed; he had a 12 year prison sentence and an unclenched thirst for revenge, come to find out his onetime best friend had crossed them.

He and Haz had a good upbringing his mother and father were married 34 years, they owned a dry cleaning business, his sister was a school teacher growing up they weren't poor like the other kids in the neighborhood nor were they rich either. He was a born hustler though from bagging groceries and selling waters as a kid to working in the barbershop as teenager.

Haz was a different breed he fell in love with the streets and the trouble it brought, he and his crew would jump other kids, steal bikes, and shoplift from stores anything they could get away with. As he got older his crew became more gangster and started robbing people, stealing cars until he finally got to the point of the robbery setup of the Jamaicans before Uncle went to jail for that lick, he was a regular young nigga from Newark looking for a way out of the ghetto just trying get a few dollars but everything changed in him in the county.

When he came home he just wanted the money, power and respect and with the street life his brother was full fledge into he saw his power and decided to get down with him, they found a cocaine connection and took their own part of the Newark dream. Now his wife was a certified junkie, his sons and Haz's son where headed down the same path of destruction as they went down. Mela was getting remarried, Haz was dead at the hands of his once best friend and to top it all off he had 7 more years in prison to do.

He was falling back in love with his first love Jahmela, He knew Clever would be a dangerous young man if he chose to use it after seeing your parents gunned down the way he had, he probably was just waiting for something to set him off but he also knew Clever was a leader not a follower.

The boys would be good they had each other F.O.E (family over everything). He had not one regret but he definitely wished he would have done a few things differently, but he had no time to think about that. It was time to holla at his man Night; it was time to find Two5.

Chapter 20

Today was Clever's 14th birthday Feb 26th, 2013. A couple of weeks had passed since his mother had gotten engaged to Devin and Clever was spending less and less time at home and more and more time with Lil Rah and Leah. Today Lil Rah, his new girl, Clever, Leah and Tah plus a couple of his crew were going down to the skating rink in Newark, Branch Brook Park Skating Rink.

Normally they would go to Skate 22 in Union, N.J. but Clever had called Night and let him know about Tah and they had a plan for him and Lil Rah wanted to scare Tah and his fake ass crew of gangster up a little. Night had told them all to come to the skating rink on Clever's birthday the plan was for everyone to have a great time, he would set up everything.

Clever went home to get dressed after he got out of the shower his mother knocked on the door of his room. (Come in Ma Clever yelled)

"Happy Birthday, baby I know you going out tonight with Leah and Lil Rah but I wanted to give you something special before you left," Mela said to her son handing him the box she had.

"What is it ma." Clever asked.

(Open it and see boy)

Clever opened the box and saw a Cuban link platinum chain with a Black Panther medallion. He put it on got up and looked in the mirror the chain looked good on him.

"It was your fathers and now it's yours, you look just like him and he was a great man but make sure you watch out for your cousins they look up to you.

"Ok Ma thank you I love the chain and I got you on everything, I'm about to go to the skate rink, I coming home tonight though" Clever said. When Clever put the chain around his neck he felt the energy and power that came with it (he didn't know what it was).but he definitely felt like the man, he called leah "I'm on my way to get you" he said, he caught a cab to Lil Rah house then they sent to pick up three girls, Rah was at the house when they left he said he would be there later one of his boy had a stolen car and him and they crew was going to meet them at the rink.

Once they got out of the cab everyone was fresh but Clever looked like money with his true religion outfit, the Cuban link around his next and Leah rolling next to him they look more like hood royalty rather than two high school kids and Lil Rah was the spitting image of his father at 13 years old be was already 5'10 looking good and his new girl was a look alike of NaNa from the movie ATL.

Night saw the chain around Clever's neck and knew he would be doing more tonight then just letting Clever know the plan about Tah he might have to hurt a nigga tonight if somebody tried his nephew, he parked his Chrysler 300c jumped out and walked over to Clever and Lil Rah "hello ladies can I talk to my nephew real quick" he said they smiled said sure we going to get our skates.

"What's good? Unk. Lil rah said to Night giving him a hood hug.

"Everything setup I got a few my young boys from around the way, I told them to start some shit tonight with Tah and his crew. No guns just a fight real hood shit if Tah crew, thorough and he really trying to be a thug then shit might get crazy if not he need to sit his little bad ass down somewhere. I wasn't going to stay from the show but you got that chain on niggas might try rob y'all so I'm going to play the background, nephews."

"Aight y'all got some young ladies in there better get in there before somebody takes them" Night said.

"Tah what up my boy" Jay said to Tah after pulling up in a stolen Dodge Caravan Jay was 14 years old, 2 years older than Tah but followed him around like a dog on a leash. Not that Jay was a follower he just had mad respect for Tah, he heard about his Uncle and father plus they were originally from Newark, they had 2 more cats in the crew Na Blood and Holla B.

Na was a fat kid 13 years old with a lot of jokes, Holla B was also 13 years old and could knock out some grown men that's how he got his name, they got in the back of the van when Tah got in.

"What's up? My nigga, where we going tonight" B said passing Tah a blunt.

"My cousin Clever having a party at Branch Brook Skating Rink, we going to go down there kick it with them fools tonight. You already know it's going to be some females there" Tah said.

When they got to the park the skating Rink was jumping you could hear the music outside cars were everywhere, they parked and went in. Tah called Lil Rah but he didn't pick up his phone they went to get some skates when he saw Leah.

"Hi, Leah where my brother and them at" Tah asked her.

"They are on the other side in the food court, you are going to see them when you get over there" Leah told him.

"What's up? Leah" Jay spoke.

"Hey Jay where you been hiding at haven't seen you at school lately" Leah said walking to the bathroom.

"They over there lets go see what's up with these fools" Tah said pointing in their direction.

"What up, Bruh Happy born day cuzzo" Tah said

"Happy born day Clever" Jay, Na and Box said dapping and hugging Clever and Lil Rah.

"Good looking y'all thanks for coming the party jumping lets go have some fun tonight" Clever said.

"Damn cuzzo that chain looking good on you, might have to hurt one these dudes in here tonight about that" Tah said.

Night sat in the game room watching Tah and his boys the next 30 minutes. It was getting close to show time his young bulls had been instigating beef with Tah and them since they showed up and it was coming close to the last skate.

(It's the last skate grab you a partner and head to the skate floor.)

(The skating rink is now closing please leave the skate floor turn in your skates and have a good night.)

Clever, Lil Rah, Leah and Kesha walked out of the skating rink, Leah called a cab. Tah and his boys were trying to get different

133

girls phone numbers; there was one Spanish girl Tah had been trying to get all night. When she walked out getting ready Tah said "Hola Mami, what's good sweetheart what's your name." She responded Mya "can I call you sometime Mami" Tah asked running his game.

"Yo little nigga why you talking to my girl get the fuck out of here before you get yourself hurt" a Spanish dude with cornrows said to Tah.

"Who the fuck you talking to what you want sauce pussy" Tah said.

Before Jay could even get over to where Tah was standing 3 other dudes were trying to surround Tah. Jay ran up on one of the dudes just as Tah swung on the first Spanish kid, Jay went at the other 3 cats just as B ran up and hit one of the dudes with a knockout punch. As soon as dude he hit the ground he was sleeping like a baby that's when the Malay broke out.

They had to be like 10 deep as they kept coming Tah noticed that Na was nowhere to be seen, where the fuck that nigga at he had to have run. Matter a fact where was his cousin and brother did them nigga leave already, Jay and B where riding kicking up on niggas but it seemed after every kick, punch there were just more dudes coming. Tah reached for his gun he had a stolen a .22 caliber about a week ago he pulled the gun out and started shooting.

Night watched Tah pull the gun as he was headed towards the fight Tah started shooting two dudes fell, the rest of them started running. Night reached Tah, at first Tah didn't realize it was his Uncle Night once Night grabbed the gun and pulled Tah, him, B and Jay ran to his car jumped in and got out of there before the cops showed up.

Night was smiling on the inside as they pulled off his nephew was definitely his father's son a future gangster.

Clever, Leah, Lil Rah and Kesha saw what was going on they saw Tah pull the gun and Night snatch him up after he started shooting. Tah was a tough Lil nigga and the streets where going to have to deal with him Clever thought.

"Damn where the fuck your brother, get a gun from" Kesha asked Lil Rah, Kesha seemed to like the gangster shit Tah had just done.

Chapter 21

6 months later.....................................

"Hey bae how was your day?" Lockout asked Tesha.

He had been rocking with Tesha a minute now, she had been around the block but she was a rider type and with all the money, beefing and shit going on in the streets right now. Lockout needed a bitch that wouldn't nut up if the pressure came down, she wasn't a gangster but Lockout taught her how to bust her gun if need be.

"My day was alright bae, besides hating ass bitches it was a normal day" Tesha ran a daycare Lockout had brought to help clean money. She didn't have to work there but she enjoyed being the boss.

"Aight come here girl" Lockout said grabbing a handful of her ass, Tesha didn't have the prettiest face but she wasn't ugly either but her ass was crazy from the back she looked like Buffy the Body or some shit. Lockout turned her around and started kissing her, kissing him back their tongues tangled in one motion he walked her back to the bed, breaking the kiss he pulled her shirt over her head. Unsnapping her bra he started sucking on her left nipple then the right one.

He made his way down he continued kissing her body, she unbuckled her pants as he pulled them down. Laying there ass naked she looked like a goddess as he parted her vaginal lips he could see her juices he tasted her slowly at first, as she started enjoying Lockout's head game she grabbed the back of his head pushing him down on her clit harder. As he worked his magic she felt herself starting to cum, she screamed oh yes daddy I'm Cumming bae, I'm Cumming yes.

Lockout kept going until he felt her body start to shake knowing that she came hard, he stood up dropped his pants and boxers down his manhood was at full attention and ready to get serviced. He stepped in from on Tesha she leaned up to grab his penis taking it into her mouth she started sucking his dick head then his balls and she went to work he was about to cum. Before he could she stopped and they got down to the business at hand.

Lockout normally wouldn't eat pussy let alone Tesha's but her head game was like super head after he would eat the box so he decided to do it today. She would take his whole dick in her mouth while tickling his balls with her tongue then she pulled back spit on his head and did it again. Damn bae damn I'm about to cum Lockout said once Tesha heard that she stopped she wanted to fuck now, she got up and bent over on the bed Lockout entered her from the back and started pounding her.

"Lockout, Lockout, yes, yes daddy beat this pussy up" Tesha screamed.

They had sex for about 30 minutes before Lockout busted his seed inside of Tesha, after that they both just laid there and fell asleep.

"Alright, my boy be safe out there them streets fucked up out there make sure you don't get into no bullshit. I ain't trying to see you back in here or on the news nigga, I'm going to be out there soon we going to link up when I touchdown" G-Money said dapping Milly because Milly would be leaving Yardville on his way back to the streets of Newark.

"Good looking bruh, I already know the shit crazy out there and I ain't thinking about coming back in this hell hole. I got to get back what I lost but I ain't never been no fool, I'm going to sit back and chill for a minute see how the streets coming before I jump back in the game. You my man I got mad love for you and if you need anything just call me and let me know, and make sure you watch your back in here. ReMo going to keep the phone I got a number in there that can always get in touch with me if you need me my boy stay sucker free" Milly told G-Money.

(Melvin Mills pack it up time to go the C.O. yelled down the tier.)

Milly Dapped G-Money "Hit me up in a few days my guy"
heading out of the cell Milly walked down the tier stopping at Re-
Mo's cell he gave him some pictures and some canteen "Hit my
phone in a week, be safe my nigga watch these clowns I'm out"
Milly said giving Re-Mo some dap and a hug "lookout for G-
Money too".

When Milly got down to the departure area, up front the C.O. gave him the clothes Christina had dropped off. He got dressed C.O. Thompson gave him a check for $1,300 the balance he had on his account, Milly signed some release paperwork and was walked out the gate towards freedom where Christina and Lockout were waiting for him in a 2013 Audi S5.

"Milly be safe out there man don't come back in this trap this is exactly where they want our people" C.O. Thompson said he was a *Black Panther he hated to see so many brothers fall into the White man trap.*

"Aight good look Thompson this definitely my last trip in a jail cell" Milly said.

Christina jumped out the driver's seat as soon as she saw Milly, she ran to him he had been like a brother to her and now that Red-Dot was dead. With Milly being locked up she had started catching feelings for him but she didn't know how he felt, as she got to him they hugged and then she kissed him and when he returned the kiss and put his tongue in her mouth she became moist. He put her down when Lockout stepped out of the car.

"What's good? My boy I been hearing a lot of good things about you out there in them streets, I hear you the man now my nigga." Milly said dapping his main man Lockout.

Lockout smiled "Naw not me I'm just a squirrel looking for a nut, I'm glad you home my boy now let's get out of this cracker ass town.

Lockout got back into the passenger seat Milly started to get into the back seat when Lockout stopped him and said "What you doing, get in the driver seat nigga you got to see how your new bitch act on the Highway."

"Word, this me nigga good looking this shit looking good my boy let me see what she can do" Milly said gassed up.

Milly jumped behind the wheel of the Audi, Christina got in the back and Milly sped off heading back to his city and his new spot next to Lockout at the top of the Throne Drug Kingpins. Since Milly had been locked up in the belly of the beast, a lot of things had changed, when Milly was out here they were getting money for Uncle Now Lockout was getting money with Uncle as an equal partner.

When Uncle was apprehended and locked up he gave Lockout the car but not the keys at first, Lockout wasn't feeling the move with Ray and the connect but now after being the man he realized exactly why Uncle did it. Shit to tell the truth he would have done the same damn thing, Uncle had long paper so he didn't want much he just needed money once in a month if that and he always wanted them to look out for his wife and the rest of his family. In the 3 years since Uncle had been gone he never missed a payment he believed in loyalty and how couldn't he be loyal to the man that put him on.

Milly pulled up to the spot Lockout opened up on Renner Ave & Bergen Street.

"Milly look you my nigga day one but shit different out here now so just take your time see what's going on before you jump back in head first, you already know your spot secure. I'm about to go upstairs I got two chicks up there waiting for you but by the way Christina was kissing you, I going to be the one have fun with them females tonight" Lockout said laughing giving Milly hood dap

"I'm out bruh hit me up when you settle in, bye Christina oh yeah Milly make sure you check the trunk I got some clothes and bread in there for you my boy peace."

Milly pulled off headed towards Christina's house he didn't know what the kiss truly meant, Chrissy was Red-Dot's girl when he got locked up but Red-Dot had been killed 2 years ago. He was loyal to his nigga but given the chance he would definitely fuck with Chrissy, he already knew she was a real down ass rider type plus she was a bad bitch best of both worlds. He was fresh out and needed to get his nuts out of the sand, minds well see what it do with Chrissy he figured he would take care of her just as Red-Dot did.

When they pulled up in front of Chrissy's house in Ivy Hill section of Newark, Milly popped the trunk grabbed the bags and followed Chrissy to the house. She opened the door and walked inside what he saw was a dope crib.

"Damn Chrissy I see you got the crib looking like a palace in this bitch." Milly told her.

"Yes I do and it is fit for a king and queen" Chrissy responded

"So, what you saying ma" Milly asked.

"I'm saying I want you I been feeling like this a while now but I didn't want to disrespect Red-Dot and I didn't know how to tell you but when I saw you earlier I knew I had to do something. When I kissed you I knew I had to tell you and when you kissed me back I knew you felt the same way." Chrissy responded.

With that all being said Milly grabbed her and started to say they couldn't but then stopped and just kissed her instead. For the next 2 hours he explored every nook and cranny of her body and by the end of their love making session Chrissy was in love with every part of Milly and that fresh home dick had her in heaven.

After putting that just came home dick down on Chrissy she when straight to sleep, Milly got up took a shower, turned the TV on and looked through the bags Lockout had given him. He found a few outfits, then he opened up the duffle bag that was also left with the other items, it was full of money he sat down at the kitchen table and started counting. Once he was finished he had counted out $185,000 he thought to himself, good look bruh that's how real niggas move.

Chapter 22

It had been 6 months since Clever's birthday party and Clever an Leah were still going together strong they had even taken each other's virginity. Their once puppy love was growing as they grew older, Lil Rah was turning into a real 13 year old ladies man. Clever still was a good student but had recently discovered a new way to get money with credit cards.

Normally he wouldn't get involved with illegal shit but it was too sweet not too and with Leah working in the mall it was too easy. He would send one of Lil Rah's many girls into Macy's where Leah worked and have them buy mad shit with the stolen credit cards.

Tah on the other hand had become a full blown young gangster with no gives a fuck, after he caught the shooting and didn't go to jail he felt untouchable. You couldn't tell him shit now he rolled even harder with Jay and B, after that night they were all mad as hell about Na so they went to his house the next day to see what was up with him.

When they got to his house his mother opened the door for them, she didn't know anything that happened so she let them in and call Na without any trouble then told them to go up to his room.

"Yo, Na where the fuck was you last night nigga them bitch ass nigga jumped us me, B, and Jay where going hard on them but you was a ghost niggas, where the fuck was you nigga" Tah asked.

"I was trying to help y'all but some big ass dudes grabbed me up, I tried to get away from them to help but they had me pinned down." Na said.

"Oh okay whatever nigga" Tah said pulling his gun **"No, No you bitch ass lying ass nigga one of the females I bagged told me you ran on us, I should shoot your faggot ass I better not see you around no more. We not friends you only alive because you mother let us in and I don't want to have to hurt her too."**

They all left out after Tah finished his speech putting the gun up Tah blew Na a kiss then made his hand look like a gun and pointed it at him.

"Night how's everything up there going, I heard Milly came home how, has he been doing" Ray asked having his usual update on the phone with Night anytime he was headed up north.

"Everything running smooth as butter, you already know Lockout still thinks he's the man. Since Milly came home he been

lying low he hasn't jumped back in the game with us yet which is a smart move. I always liked Milly more than Lockout; he always seemed like the smart one of the two. The feds moving Uncle to P.A. next week, I'm going to go and visit him got a lot to talk to him about."

"Tah out here going off in the streets out here moving like he trying be the future king, he coming like he in a gangster movie or some shit. But other than that everything is everything the trap still Gucci and the blocks still jumping like always. What about on your end?" Night asked

"Everything green down here on my end, since I have been fucking with the home boy down here we done locked down some new spots. We in Decatur, Bankhead and we are moving into Savannah and Albany, G.A. Plus we opened up a strip club down here too, and shit doing numbers too it's called Ladies Paradise. All bad bitches, all these rappers and balled niggas be in here every night trying to make it rain and shit."

"On another note I will be up there next week so wait for me before you go to visit Uncle. I'm going to go with you I have to discuss a few things as well, Night I love you my nigga watch that nigga Lockout make sure he don't try to switch up and shit now that his man home cause he will get it too" Ray said.

It had been 2 weeks since Ray talked to Night he was supposed to be up North now but his and Kevin's club Ladies Paradise was making too much noise in the Atlanta area so he couldn't leave yet. Plus he didn't want to leave the business in the hands of Kev yet so he waited for a little down time that came the next week. When Kevin's artist I.B. was in the club chilling with his entourage and fellow rapper Showtimeleek and his crew came into the club.

I.B. was from Newark, N.J. and Showtimeleek had just dissed the entire state of N.J. The Grape Street Crips had already told Showtimeleek what it was if they caught him so I.B. could careless; fuck that whack ass nigga he thought.

"Yo, there that nigga Showtimeleek I should go smack that boy, talking all that tough rap shit." I.B. man Eli said.

Another hour or so went by when Eli noticed somebody from Showtimeleek's crew pointing at I.B. and with that he got up headed in their direction when I.B. noticed where Eli was going he and the rest of his crew followed.

"Fuck you pointing at nigga" Eli said to the one that was pointing at them then he looked at Showtimeleek "What's up with that entire blow up New Jersey shit Lil boy" with those words one of the niggas in Showtimeleek's crew got up and swung on Eli. Next thing you knew it was mayhem in Paradise cats got hit with fist, bottles, and chairs before it was all over somebody fired 4 shots nobody got hit or even saw the shooter.

The beef was definitely on now the cops showed up shut the club down for the night; they talked to a few people got very little information and left as fast as they arrived.

As they waited for the heat to die down, Ray headed up top to Newark he was a week behind, he had to go pick up weight and still wanted to go see Uncle.

"I will be there in a few hours, I'm at the airport now" Ray said after calling Night. 4 hours later Night was outside of Newark Liberty Airport waiting for Ray to come outside.

"What's up? Ray how's the club business treating you, I saw the news so you got rappers shooting up the club now" Night said laughing.

"Yeah shit got crazy down there that night I.B. and his crew saw that Showtimeleek nigga, you know the one that dissed Jersey. So you know it went down after that" Ray said laughing himself.

2 hours later Night and Ray pulled up in front of USP Canaan in Waymart, Pennsylvania. Heading to see Uncle this was the first time either one of them visited but they knew Uncle would be glad to see them. Most of the time your homies never came to visit you in jail at all.

Night and Ray stepped inside the prison "we are here to visit Rashaan Anderson" Ray told the clerk at the front desk.

"Okay fill out this visit card and walk this way" the C.O at the desk informed them checking their names on Uncle's visit list.

"Rashaan Anderson you have a visit, Rashaan Anderson visit" the C.O yelled down the tier.

Uncle was surprised he talked to Jahmela she wasn't coming to see him this week, so he had no idea who was coming to visit him this time around. Uncle got himself together put on his visit uniform and headed out of his cell. When Uncle walked on the visit floor he was looking around trying to figure out who was visiting him, when he saw Night and Ray he got concerned.

He couldn't figure out why they came to visit him but when they saw him they both smiled, which relieved some of the stress he was having at the time. (Uncle walked over to them)

"What's good? Big man damn I see you in here on your workout shit nigga" Night said to Uncle when he walked up.

"What's good? Cuzzo" Ray said standing up to hug Uncle.

"Shit I'm doing okay, what you two fools doing down here" Uncle asked.

"Damn we can't come visit the family in the box, what you want us to leave" Night said laughing at Uncle.

"Shit nigga we came to check on you it has been a while we needed to update you on the outside world, my man business going good and your young bull Milly came home a few weeks ago" Night said.

"I'm just messing with y'all, I'm glad to see you two guys so what has been going on out there in the free world. I just got some fucking good news about my case; I got a chance to get my sentence reduced next month. My Lawyer says I got a great chance to get this 12 years reduced to 8 years maybe even 7 years, I got 3 years in already so 8 would put me at about 4 more years to go" Uncle told him.

"Oh shit that's some good ass news that's what I'm talking about these crackers can't keep a good man down. Rah business been great I'm down south locking more shit down with my new partner Kev, we got a club in Atlanta called Ladies Paradise. We moving work in a couple of spots down there too." Ray said

"Hold on, Hold on I seen some shit on the news about that club getting shot up by some rap beef or some shit." Uncle said

"Yeah, Yeah that was us them rap niggas I.B. and Showtimeleek saw each other, they were beefing over that disrespect about Jersey and shit went down when they saw each other. But fuck all that bullshit I came to ask you if your boy Milly good, Lockout said he want him to get down back with the business up here. I don't know him but he's your man so I need to get your confirmation before I fuck with him." Ray said

"Oh yeah, that young boy different Milly good bread real stand up dude. If he was out there when I took my fall I would have giving him the position I put Lockout in, so whenever he ready put him on you don't got to worry about him. So you got a new partner I don't know shit about son but you definitely need to be watching him at all times. You already know the Feds are everywhere and shooting in the club could bring a lot of unwanted unnecessary attention to you" Uncle said

"Yeah you already know I was on that nigga like a cheap suit I had my cop friend check Kev out he good from everything I found out plus son from Newark he been down the A for a minute now though." Ray informed Uncle and Night.

"So what about you Night, what has been going on you mighty quiet over there and shit what's good brother" Uncle asked Night.

"Everything, Everything on my end I been playing your boys heavy lately but they good Lil Rah just like you he think he the fleetest nigga in the city. Now that damn Tah he a whole other story, he a

straight goon like Haz use to be when we was coming up." Night said laughing.

Night told Uncle about the shooting at Clever's birthday party, he told him everything except the part about him and Clever setting the whole fight thing up.

"Clever been doing all kinds of credit card and check scams he think he low and I don't know, but you already know the streets do more talking than a female. Lil Rah and Clever still going to school every day but Tah do whatever he want, I try to be there for them but I'm not you so they only listen when they want too. Gina back getting high so they basically raising themselves, Jahmela and Mela be on they ass too but you already know how it go we all been where them boys at now" Night said finishing his tale.

"Alright Night just stay on they ass and try to bring them to see me, I need to talk to all of them. But I'm glad y'all came to see me I been having some information but I didn't really know what to do or how to do it but I found out who killed Haz." Uncle said

Ray damn near yelled to the top of his lungs "Who is it time for niggas to bleed."

"That's the thing I been fucked up about Night, remember Two5 from back in the day I use to roll with him he was my day

one best friend. Jahmela came to see me about 6 months ago and told me Milly got a parole date and that he and G-Money was cell mates down the Ville, Milly finally got G-Money to slip up. He gave up the information about the Robbery on Haz and Mela.

Milly told her that Two5 set it all up when he came home a while back and G-Money, and Rock did the shit. They were supposed to just rob them or some shit but Rock said G-Money name so they had to kill them and then G-Money killed Rock that same night." Uncle told both of them.

"Yeah I remember son he use to fuck with Mela right before he got bagged and then Haz started fucking with her. Tell truth nigga probably was still mad about that, plus he got like 10 years from that robbery shit they all did back in the day." Night said.

"Word, so what I need you to do Night is see if we can find this nigga. I heard he been a ghost nobody ain't supposedly seen him since he been home but I know you can find out something. Oh yeah and send word down the Ville put a price on the nigga G-Money head it's time he go meet his maker too." Uncle said.

(Visits are over all inmates' line up it's time to exit the visit floor.)

"Alright bruh enough said it's a done deal" Night said getting up to hug Uncle.

153

"Stay up cuzzo love that nigga, everything going to get handle we on it" Ray said hugging Uncle as well.

Chapter 23

3 months later.............................

Time had been flying by in a blink of an eye it seemed like yesterday that Clever had started fucking with the credit card scams. Now he was a full fledge scammer getting money off checks, money orders, Ebay and Paypal, all while maintaining a 3.0 GPA. Clever was a hustler to the core but still had dreams of going to college one day, but as of now his goals were all focused on getting money.

His newest scam was in the banks today he had 2 dudes who wanted to put checks in their accounts once they cleared he would split the money with them. They met at the Bank of America, Clever walked to the car they were in and handed them two checks. He told them to put them in each of their accounts and give him their debit cards before they went in the bank. The checks where certified so they would clear almost instantly, so they should come out of the bank with $3500 a piece to be split with Clever.

Clever waited outside when the two came back out they were both laughing, Clever saw the money envelopes so he knew everything went well. As he met the two at their car he got into it, they gave

Clever $200 pulled a gun and said get the fuck out of here little nigga. You lucky we gave you anything my man here was just gone shoot your stupid ass. (Laugh, Laugh)

Clever jumped out of the car, he was heated mad as hell but he couldn't do anything about it right now. They had a gun and numbers 2 to 1, they won this round but Clever promised himself he would never be caught slipping again.

Clever left and called Lil Rah "yo cuzzo I just got robbed."

"What nigga fuck you mean by who where you at I'm with Tah now where you at we on the way" Lil Rah said into the phone on fire.

"Naw, Naw, cuzzo I'm on my way to your house now meet me there." Clever said.

Milly had been out now about 3 months, him and Chrissy where fast becoming a team. At first he thought it wouldn't work out but they were actual good together, she was a boss bitch and he had always been a boss nigga he had jumped back in the game the pass month. Lockout was the man now so things were different, he now worked for Lockout.

He didn't really care who the boss was but he knew Lockout and wasn't trying to be under him to long. He knew he would fuck up eventually and he wasn't trying to go back to jail for the company he kept, while Chrissy paid the bill he saw a kid he could have sworn was Clever Uncle's nephew. He wasn't sure it had been a long while since he had seen Clever or Uncle's sons.

He couldn't be sure he started to go see but then thought better of it when he saw the two other boys approach the kid and jump in a car. He saw the two other boys say something to the kid and one of them pointed a gun at him, the Clever look a-like didn't finch he said something but stood his ground until the car pulled off .

"Earth to Milly damn bae what you over their looking at" Chrissy asked him.

"I don't know look like that little nigga right there just got robbed or something, niggas pulled a strap on him" Milly said.

"Damn that's fucking crazy for real, for real" Chrissy said pulling out of the parking lot.

Milly had to kept his word and was holding G-Money down; Uncle never said anything about G-Money after he told him about Two5. G-Money was still alive so he figured Uncle didn't care about G, G-Money was sitting in his cell smoking when Re-Mo came in.

"What up G-Money let me hit that shit, did you hear from Milly lately I been calling him last few days ain't heard shit from him" Re-Mo said.

"Yeah I talked to him last week he said, he had to change his number" G-Money said.

"Oh okay alright if you talk to him tell him I need to holla at him a.s.a.p. it's important" Re-Mo said.

Re-Mo had recently gotten word down the prison that G-Money was a wanted man; somebody had put $5,000 on his head. They wanted to make sure he didn't make it out of prison in 12 months, from the information he received a nigga named Night was behind the hit. The streets said Night was rolling with Lockout and Re-Mo remembered hearing Milly talk about Lockout a few times, but he wanted to get a little more information before he made his move.

He never really liked the nigga G-Money anyway, so he definitely was trying to cash out on that nigga.

"What up? Cuzzo what the fuck happened, who the fuck robbed you them niggas died" Lil Rah said mad as hell.

"Word I met these two cats online they wanted to do business with me, so I hollered at them to set everything up. I met them at the bank I gave them the checks to bust they went in and

busted them, when they came out they gave me $200 pulled a strap and told me get the fuck out of here little nigga before I shoot you. Once they pulled the gun I jumped out the car."

"All I know about them niggas is there online pages, I checked them shits they deleted them already. They got that for now but I going to win, where Tah at." Clever asked.

"He left he said he will be back for you to wait for him until he get back" Lil Rah said.

Milly had been waiting for Night to meet him at the Ramada Inn in East Orange, N.J. They had gotten accustomed to meeting once in a while since Milly had gotten back in the game with them. Normally Lockout would attend the meetings but he was out of town handling business on another front, so tonight it would be just Milly and Night holding the fort down.

When Night pulled into the parking lot, Milly could see he had a passenger in the car upon getting closer to him. Milly noticed the passenger was the same kid from earlier he saw outside the bank the kid must have been Clever, Milly thought.

"What's up? Night what it do O.G." Milly said dapping him up "Who the kid I saw him earlier at the bank"

"This is Clever, Uncle's nephew this my little man he got robbed today he called me told me what happened. He told me niggas robbed him at the back for 3 racks but what I'm trying to figure out is where he got 3 racks from. He doesn't know I know what he into now, doing all kinds of scams and shit. You said you saw him earlier what did you see Milly." Night asked

"I don't really know I saw him, I thought he looked like Uncle then I thought it was Clever but I haven't seen him in a while so I said fuck it. After that I saw two cats come out the bank jump in a Dodge Charger pull a gun say something to him and pull off. I could tell he was mad and wanted sauce but he was smart enough to know he couldn't win right now. So he just stood there then Chrissy jumped in the car and we left." Milly told Night.

"Aight Milly you the youngest nigga in our circle, I trust you, Uncle trust you so I want you to watch out for the boys. They all at the age where they finding themselves and you a real nigga so they need to be around somebody like you" Night said.

"True, true, you already know, what's good young bull I saw you I know you got heart and you ain't any dumb nigga. If you ever need me just call your father looked me out when I was your age coming up, so I will always do the same thing." Milly told Clever.

"Aight bruh cool good looking I'm going to hit you up; I remember you my father use to talk about you and Lockout." Clever said.

"Okay todays meet and greet is over, I didn't have anything to talk to you about Milly. I was going to cancel until Clever called me and told me about the robbery, when Lockout get back Ray going to come up and we can all sit down then. Be safe hit my jack if you need me peace" Night said getting back in his car; he pulled out the parking lot headed towards Clever's house.

G-Money sat in his cell staring at the underneath of the top bunk, he was lost in his thoughts he was getting short he had less than a year to do. He was thinking about what his plan was going to be once he was released, he had no plans on doing any robberies. He was done robbing niggas but he wasn't a drug dealer either and working wasn't going to work, so he would have to do at least one more robbery. He was running out of money fast, as he thought about what he had to do he kept coming back to robbing Milly and going down south.

What happens in the streets normally hits the jails fast and the word was Milly was back at it and getting real money out there. Plus he put 3 racks on his books and 2 racks on Re-Mo's books so he definitely was out there getting money.

(Rec out, rec out last call for the gym.)

G-Money heard the call for the Rec yard snapping him out of his day dream, he grabbed his Walkman caught his cell door and headed out. He bumped into another inmate as he exited his cell, G-Money started to say watch out nigga when he saw the inmate had his face covered with a mask and a shank in his hand. He pushed G-Money back into his cell and started stabbing him, G-Money hit the back of his bunk he fought back but dude had already hit him twice and was big a shit. He caught him off guard G-Money tried to yell but nothing came out as the dude continued to poke him up.

He realized his only option was to fake dead and hope the dude stopped stabbing him and left, as he crumbled to the cell floor the inmate stabbed him one more time and said die you bitch ass nigga. I never liked you anyway fuck nigga, hearing the voice he realized it was Re-Mo, he walked out the cell closed the door and left G-Money on the floor bleeding.

G-Money wasn't ready to die but he had been stabbed over 15 times and life was leaving him right there on the cell floor, G-Money tried to crawl to the door. He started banging on the door but his cell was in the back of the tier and everybody was at rec so nobody could hear him banging.

G-Money's Cell mate had just got off work in the kitchen, he was about to go to rec but then decided to go back on the tier and get in the shower and jump on the phone. When he got on the tier he told the C.O. to pop his cell, when he got to his cell door he looked in the window he saw the cell empty. He was glad G-Money went to rec so he could have the cell to his self, when the C.O. popped the door he stepped in the cell almost slipping and falling.

He caught his balance looked down and saw blood everywhere; G-Money was crumpled on the floor. "C.O., C.O.," G-Money's Bunkie ran up front telling them my Bunkie got stabbed up or some shit he on the floor bleeding its blood everywhere.

The officers on duty ran down the tier took one look at G-Money on the floor, and radioed in we have an assault on South 2 A wing. Inmate is on the floor bleeding heavy looks to be a stabbing multiple times. Still alive and bleeding heavily.

The medical team got to G-Money in 10 minutes strapped him to a gurney, assessed him and decided he needed to be helicopter to Robert Wood Johnson Hospital in Trenton, N.J. G-Money was still hanging on to life, all he could think about is why this happened and if

Milly had something to do with it. Re-Mo was Milly's man he didn't

know but if he survived he would find out.

Chapter 24

Lockout had been going back and forth to Ohio the past 4 to 5 months; he had family out there in Youngstown and Cleveland. He had been getting money out there lately shit was different out here with these Midwest boys they sold shit in break offs not bottles or baggies but prices were higher out there. Lockout was hitting his cousin with keys at 26 a bird, $5,000 more then he sold them for in Jersey plus he was cutting the work and made 2 out of 1 brick so he was winning all the way around.

"Cuzzo, what's good? We need 10 this time but I need a better price I can do 23 a bird" Lockout's cousin said in his Ohio accent.

Lockout hadn't seen his cousin in 12 years since when his uncle moved out to Ohio, but his aunt had gotten sick and Lockout came to visit them at the request of his mother. Once he got out there his cousin hollered at him about the drugs and it was on from there. Lockout never thought to ask his cousin how he knew his business, the prices he was giving his cousin was too good so he ignored things he should have been watching.

"I only have 7 with me, I can give you those for 24 apiece the best I can do until I go back home. I will throw you 3 on

consignment when I get back Lil cuzzo. You know I got you F.O.E (Family Over Everything) one love, I will bring you the 7 later tonight I'm out" Lockout said dapping his cousin before leaving.

After the shooting at the club Ladies Paradise had become the hot spot to be at in Atlanta again damn near overnight, Kevin and Ray boosted up security. Kevin had been making more money than he had ever done before Ray had become a god send to him he was a good connect but an even better business partner. Kevin had been in the streets a long time and he had distanced himself since he had been home, lately he had been thinking about Mela.

She had survived the gunshot wound and was getting remarried soon he heard Clever was growing into a smart young man. He wished he could see her but he knew that wasn't possible, he was sure nobody knew about his involvement in Haz's murder but he couldn't risk it. Plus he recently heard about G-Money getting stabbed up in prison.

"What's up? Kev" Ray said walking in to his office.

When Ray entered his office it brought to his mind he hadn't heard from his friend in Newark that he had check on Ray, he made a mental note to call him back later.

(Ray noticed the slight Kev gave when he asked him what up but he brushed it off.)

"We have some rap crews coming in tonight, they want us to shut the club down and make it a private party for them. I wanted to talk to you about how much you want to charge them, on a normal Friday night we do about 25 thousand between the door, bar and the dancers. So I was thing we charge them 30k for the night." Ray said

"I was thinking just charge them 20k and make sure you tell them to tip our ladies real good, we can let tonight be about the dancers. We can let them make the money tonight" Kev said.

Kev said he was thinking like Two5 again, he figured keep the ladies happy and they will remain loyal plus they had a few dancers that nigga came to the club to see. He knew other clubs had been trying to steal some of their best earning females and he wasn't having that.

"If that's all you need I have to go out to take care of a few things, I will be back" Kevin said getting up he wanted to make the call about Ray while he remember, he had a feeling something was off about Ray.

"Listen Jamal we have been working with you for 6 months now, you got caught with 3 kilos of Cocaine coming across the

Ohio/Pennsylvania border lines you are looking at a lot of time. You will be going to the Federal Prison system unless you give us something now not tomorrow. We have given you plenty of time and chances to help yourself, we want your cousin not you."

"He is one of the biggest drug traffickers in this country and we want him but your time is running out Jamal you have until the end of the week. We want him on recording selling you drugs or you are going to be in jail and not him." Federal Agent Davenport said.

"Look, look man I got him delivering me 7 kilos tonight just tap my phone or some shit. When I call him to see what time he coming y'all can get him on tape and be at the spot to arrest him too" Jamal Lockout's cousin said.

"For your benefit you better hope and pray he shows up but you will have to wear a wire. An make sure you say his name and what you are buying loud and clear" Agent Davenport said pointing at Jamal.

"Okay I got you" make the call you rat bastard Agent Davenport's partner Agent Matthews said to Jamal.

Even though Agent Matthews was a cop he hated to see other black men snitching on another, the stupid niggas didn't even realize they made a lot of the case for them. When they told on each other they made cases for the police and Jamal was the worst kind of snitch he was setting up his own family. His own flesh and blood, so much for family over everything.

"Okay he said we going to meet at the Marriot tonight at 11pm" Jamal said.

Kevin called his contact in Jersey, Winston an ex Newark Police turned bodyguard to the stars. (Ring, Ring)

"Hello who's this" Winston asked when he answered the private number.

"It's Two5 I meant to call you about the information I asked for but I got sidetracked. What's going on Winston did you get any information on Ray Jones." Two5 asked.

"Yeah Two5 I got something doesn't help much but you paid for it let me check my files. Alright here I got it your man Ray was raised by Crystal Jones, his aunt they lived in Florida 10 years. He has no record, no kids, no wife, no siblings, 2 cousins Kamela Anderson and Jahmela Jones, he pretty much is clean few petty arrest as a kid nothing since. So it looks like your associate is clear." Winston told Two5.

Two5 didn't hear anything after Winston said he had 2 cousins Kamela Anderson and Jahmela Jones, Ray his new business partner and connect was family with Mela, he was Haz family. But now he was around him his brain was spinning did Ray know who he was, did he know about the murder, was he here to set him up.

Kevin didn't know what was going on but going back to his instincts he would become Two5 again. He was going to come up with a plan to get rid of Ray before Ray could make a move on him.

"Okay Winston thanks for the help take care" Two5 said before hanging up the phone.

Damn I knew something was up with this nigga Ray I guess Rah must've sent this nigga at me. When Mela woke up she had to tell him about Rock saying G-Money name and somehow they got the information about him from G-Money. That has to be why G-Money got stabbed up, well fuck it it's time for his partner to become his ex-business partner.

"Lockout lets go back to the hood, I'm tired of this country ass town and your country ass cousins. Fuck that little bit of extra money, you know we don't need it we good come on bae let's just go home." Tasha begged him she was ready to go home; she had been trying to get Lockout to leave since they got here. She didn't like the vibe out here or his cousin Jamal.

"Alright bae let me make this drop-off then we can bounce love" Lockout said to her girl.

"Okay gentlemen here comes the target, he is in a BMW X5 black with dark tinted windows. The show is on let him come in the room make the transaction and when he leaves we will grab him up. Jamal it's your time to shine lets go" Agent Davenport said

"What's good? Cuzzo how them birds looking same as before right I hope so the price $24,000 a piece right" Jamal asked Lockout.

"Yeah cuzzo here the coke, give me the money I'm out got to get back to Jersey" Lockout said dapping Jamal.

"Aight cuzzo here the bread it's $168,000 be safe, I'm going to hit you when I need to re-up" Jamal said dapping his cousin back.

Lockout left the room and head back to the lobby, when Lockout got to the lobby he could sense something was off. As soon as he jumped off the elevator he saw two white boys looking in his direction. He wasn't stupid he could tell they were looking at him but trying not to be seen, that's when Tesha words came to his mind I don't trust your cousin.

Then he started thinking how did his cousin even know that he sold weight as soon as he got to Ohio, because as soon as he got there his cousin Jamal was trying to cop from him. He made a split second decision; this had to be a setup he slipped out a side door now he could see cop cars everywhere he had to figure out something. He texted Tesha, who was still in the car and told her plan b.

Two5 went back to the club trying to figure out how he was going to handle the whole situation with Ray, should he just kill him or do more watching of him. He truly liked Ray he didn't want to kill him but he knew in the back of his mind it was either Ray or him and he always choose himself. By the time he entered the club he had come up with the perfect plan.

He pulled up in front of the club it was packed like sardines as always, the valet ran to his car. "What's up? Boss man" the valet said before parking his car. Two5 walked into the club spotted the hottest new rap crew the Migos; he headed to his office and sat in his office until the club shut down.

(Last call for Alcohol)

It was now Showtime he waited 20 minutes to make sure the club was empty; he checked the camera's saw everything was clear. Ray was in his office with one of the new girls, Candy or Lollipop, Two5 hadn't met her yet he planned on making it look like a robbery

172

gone bad. He wished the girl wasn't there but she would have to pay for Ray's sins as well. When he walked into Ray's office he was sitting behind his desk while Candy was on her knees servicing him.

She was facing away from Two5 so he decided she might be useful alive, he had found a mask but before he pulled it down Ray saw him. Ray thought nothing of Two5 coming into his office until he saw the mask being pulled over his face. Before Ray could do anything Two5 shot him 3 times in the head then went into his act "Bitch get up where is the money".

"I don't know nothing I just started working here this my first week, please don't kill me" Candy screamed in fear.

He hit her in the back of the head with the gun, as she fell to the floor passed out he made his way to the security room to take all of the video footage.

Chapter 25

1 Year Later...

It had been exactly 14 months since Ray's murder and a lot had changed in that time. Clever still was going to school and doing scams on the side, Mela had finally walked down the aisle. Lil Rah was still a sometimes good 15 year old kid but the biggest change came in Tah, Ray was the closest to him and when Ray was murdered he took to the streets and hustling much harder and better.

With no parents to try and stop him he became a natural born go getter, the one good thing Uncle still had was Jahmela. They had become a couple once again; they were going strong and any day now Uncle would get the ruling on his attempt at being resentenced.

As Uncle sat in his cell his thoughts wandered back to the day he found out about Ray's murder and what it meant for him and the rest of his family.

(Anderson, Anderson Legal mail, and sign here I have to open it up the C.O. said delivering Uncle the legal mail.)

Uncle got the envelope from the C.O. read the letter to himself Rashaan Anderson your Attorney's have filed a motion on your behave to ask for reconsideration of your sentence. We are currently examining your case and will be letting you know of our decision in the near future. Uncle looked at the letter already knowing all the information it stated but was still happy to see it in writing.

Next Day after shooting.................................

(Breaking News in Atlanta, G.A. new channel 10 reporting live the owner of an exotic night club named Ladies Paradise was shot and killed last night while in his office last night after the club had closed down for the night. It looks to be a robbery gone wrong; a witness who is not being identified says a masked man broke into the club shot her boss Raymond Jones about 3 times in the head and face region. Mr. Jones' family has been notified and is arriving as we speak.

Co-Owner Kevin Lockette is currently arriving right now; let's see if we can get a word with him.

(When Uncle saw the man identified as the Co-Owner Kevin Lockette he saw red, he looked older and bigger but it was definitely Two5.)

"Ray was a great man and will be extremely missed by me and many more people including his family and friends. God rest his soul I pray they find the ones who did this no further comments" Two5 said walking inside of the club.

(Back to you Melissa, this is Gary Owens live at Ladies Paradise.)

It didn't take much for Uncle to put 2 and 2 together what he thought probably happened was Ray must've not known who his business partner really was. And somehow Two5 had to know about whom Ray was and killed him or had him killed. Two5 had to go he was now up 2 to 0, something had to give.

Ray was dead, Lockout was on the run from the Feds and G-Money had survived the stabbing seems like nothing was going his way.

Uncle had to figure out something as his thoughts came back to the present he thought about the news, he recently got from Night. G-Money was home now he thought about what he wanted to do about that.

1 month later………………………….

"Damn G you been home less than a month and you ain't taking no breaks, I see you ain't playing no games out here, you playing for keeps my nigga. What's the real deal my boy we doing juxes damn near every day and we only robbing the boy Milly spots. What's good with that? I'm not complaining, I'm just curious why only

Milly when it's hella niggas out here getting to that bag we could be getting" G-Money's man Wise asked.

"We hitting his spots because he sweet plus it's been working, he was my Bunkie, my dude down the building but he set me up. He the reason I got stabbed up down the Ville by his man, when he left they put me on a plate I wasn't sure until I got out though. I found out he was getting money with the boy Uncle, it all made sense he never said shit about the nigga though down prison.

Now I come home and he the man, nigga tried to cash in on me so your already know I'm robbing every nigga he roll with till I can get at him. Plus any nigga he rolls with need to be touched anyway. G-Money said.

Wise knew it was something wrong, he thought something was missing because G-Money never said why he had a problem with Uncle. He thought he knew why but he did know Uncle was a good nigga the streets said all good things about him, he passed out toys on Christmas, Turkeys on Thanksgiving he was a real standup dude. He looked out for a lot of people.

"Oh alright Gee you already know I'm with you till the end, let's get this money. I more than hungry matter fact I'm starving my guy" Wise said being extra.

"I have a plan to get one big payday then we can fall back forever plus take a vacation or something. Uncle put Milly in charge since Lockout went on the run, Night was his number 2 man then you have a few other cats not really important but here. What I'm thinking is Uncle has 2 sons Lil Rah, and Tah plus his nephew Clever. I think we just snatch up one them little niggas, hold them for ransom I know Night gone pay for anyone of them little niggas. Uncle wouldn't have it any other way." G-Money said.

(Anderson, Anderson, Attorney Visit the C.O. yelled down the tier.)

"Hello, Rashaan his attorney Mr. Rosenberg said I have some good news for you that's why I showed up to tell you in person. You are scheduled to leave this faculty next week; you are going back to Essex County Correctional Faculty, where you have a hearing coming up in about 2 weeks about your motion for a reduction in your sentence. The way it is looking as of now you will be granted the reduction but we can't be 100 percent, but it looks as if you will go from 12 years to 8 years we will still push for a reduction to 7 years though."

"We will need another payment at the end of the hearing but other than that you are all set and it looks as if you will be a free man pretty soon, Good Luck Rashaan." Uncle's lawyer informed him of all the good news.

"Great, Great sounds like a fucking plan Rosenberg" Rah said getting up and shaking his lawyer's hand. Wasn't anything else to talk about, "See you next week have a good one" Rah left the room headed to the phones to call Jahmela. Now that he would be headed to the County he could make a few more moves, while he was there.

(Ring, Ring, You have a prepaid call from Rashaan Anderson, Press 1 to accept. Jahmela pressed 1 as soon as she heard the automated message.)

"Hey bae I'm at work only got a little while to talk. What's going on?" Jahmela asked Uncle.

"Okay bae my lawyer just left from visiting me down here, he said my motion was granted and I have a hearing coming up next week. He also said I got a great chance at 8 years but they still are pushing for 7 years, he needs another $5,000 but I need you to tell Night and Milly to come see me. When I get to the county, I'm going to let you know but go ahead and get back to work bae I love you, I will see you next week." Uncle said.

1 week later...

Uncle had a lot to think about causing a week to seem like overnight, in a blink of an eye it was time for him to be transported back to the Essex County Jail in Newark. This is the same place his journey began almost 5 years ago; he had a lot to handle now that his freedom was so close at hand. If his court hearing went the way he wanted, he could be a free man in about a year and a half; he couldn't let anything interfere with that so he thought about what he still knew had to be done on the outside before he could truly become a free man.

He knew that even though Lockout hadn't snitched yet it was only a matter of time before he was caught and the feds started throwing them football numbers at him. He would do as all self-proclaimed real niggas did, then there was the issue of G-Money he had survived the murder attempt and common sense should give him a clue as to where the attempt came from. An then there was Two5 out there in Atlanta just living his best life as a free man with businesses plus who knows what else he was up to, one thing for sure he had to go.

(Rashaan Anderson, Rashaan Anderson pack it up time to go the C.O. yelled)

"What's good? Uncle what it do" another inmate said as Rah walked on the Federal inmate holding pad in the Essex County Correctional Faculty.

"What it do my guy" Ab said to Uncle.

"Chilling Man trying to fight these crackers man they trying to give me 30 to life, I told them come talk to me when they sober" Ab said laughing and dapping Uncle.

"I hear that shit my boy, I'm here trying to give these pussy ass crackers this time back myself I need to get the fuck out" Uncle told Ab.

"I hear you playboy shit crazy I know so I'm going to let you get settled in but I need to holler at you. It's a lot going on out there in them streets with your young boy Milly and that nigga G-Money, but anyway I'm on the top tier in cell 10 come holler at me. When you done my boy come through, glad to see you even though we both in this situation. Wish we both were under different circumstances but it is what it is destined to but Allah knows best" Ab said.

After dropping off his stuff in his cell and meeting his Bunkie, a young cat around 19 named D-West he headed back to Ab's cell.

"What's shaking? Ab what the fuck going on I need to know." Uncle asked.

"As I already said it's about your man Milly, shit crazy his spots and some of his runners been getting robbed damn near every day. I don't know what he did to G-Money but from what I hear they were Bunkie's down the Ville and now since G-Money been home him and his man Wise been shaking shit. From what I'm hearing he only shaking Milly's block, I'm only telling you because we go back a while and I know you fuck with the boy Milly" Ab said.

"Good looking my nigga you already know I'm going check into all this shit" Uncle said to Ab.

After getting the newest 411 Uncle went straight to the phones, (Ring, Ring, Hello you have a collect call from Rashaan Anderson to accept press 5. Jahmela pressed 5 as soon as the call went though.)

"Hey, bae I just got to the county jail bae visits are tomorrow I put you on the list already, I need you to come see me," they talked until the 15 minute call ended then Uncle called Milly he accepted the call "Milly this Uncle I need you to come see me tomorrow, I'm in the county now we got a lot to talk about" Uncle said before he hung up.

Chapter 26

Clever was chilling today with Leah, Lil Rah, Tah and both of their girls. They all planned on going to the movies today but nobody could agree on what to go see so they changed plans and decided to just chill at the house. Clever had gotten his first scholarship offer and they all wanted to celebrate the achievement.

He now was carrying a gun just like his little cousin Tah after Milly told him about the danger, he and the rest of them might be in. Milly knew Uncle wouldn't approve of him giving Clever a gun, but once he told Clever about G-Money shooting his father Clever realized it was the only option.

Plus he knew Uncle would rather they be able to protect themselves if something went down than not too. Tah was already a great shot marksman type shit, Clever was ok but Lil Rah didn't like guns he said to many black kids where dying because of them.

(Ring, Ring)

"Aye Night, Uncle just called he said he in the county now about to give some time back he want us to come visit him tomorrow" Milly told Night after he hung up the phone.

"Shit that's good news but I can't make it to visit, I have some information on them robberies we been experiencing and I have to go check on it a.s.a.p. Tomorrow is the perfect day no time to waste tell Uncle I see him next time" Night said already knowing Rah was coming to the county.

"Okay big bruh go handle that shit I will go see Uncle by myself, stay up love that nigga" Milly said dapping Night.

"Love that nigga back you already know the shit" Night said

Behind the limo tint of his rental 2012 Dodge Charger, he could still see the kids in the back yard of Gina's house. He had been following them for 6 days and had yet to see Gina, word was she was a full-fledged crackhead now and rarely ever came home. The kids were basically raising themselves, he could tell Clever was the smart one, the leader Lil Rah followed Clever and loved the young ladies but Tah he was a future boss a real gangster.

If anyone tried them he definitely would be a problem, he had noticed a Mazda MPV silver with tinted windows the past few days and as it rode by again he decided to follow it, he followed it at a safe distance the driver must've noticed him following them because it took off speeding away. Now he knew he had a problem somebody else was watching the kids also, he wasn't 100% sure but he would go with his first instinct. Whoever was behind the wheel of that van wanted Clever and/or Lil Rah and Tah.

G-Money and Wise had been watching the kids and Milly, Milly wasn't a fool he knew something was off so he stayed on alert. He visited the boys a lot now so G-Money figured he was expecting something and now there was another hiccup, there had been a black Dodge Charger watching the house too. G-Money had no idea who was in the car, could be the police or anybody else for that matter.

For his plan to go off right he had to find out who was in the Dodge Charger but before he could get the chance it started following them. As they cruised through the block on their final dry run, he wanted to get them at the house because he knew he could get all of them if he struck at their house. They would be less on guard he thought, tonight was supposed to be show time but they would have to wait until tomorrow to figure out everything new.

(Rashaan Anderson visit, visit Rashaan Anderson)

Uncle walked into the visit booth where Milly was already sitting waiting for him.

"As-Salam-u-Alaikum" Uncle said greeting Milly.

"Wa-Alaikumussalam Wa-Rahmatullah" Milly responded to Uncle "What's going on Uncle?"

"I should be asking you that question from what I hear you taking major loses, getting robbed daily and nothing happening to the people who doing the robbing. I don't know if you can't handle being the boss or if you just went soft but from what I hear G-Money waging war on you and he still breathing. I say since he's still alive my sons are at risk." Uncle said to Milly a little upset.

"Naw, Naw, Oh G I can assure you I'm the same boss nigga you raised me to be and I would never let anything happen to the boys. Yeah the boy G-Money been a real problem I got money on his head, plus I got my young boys out there charging him but he been like a ghost right now. He hit the spots and then disappears, I talked to Night he said he got some information on the nigga that's why he didn't show up today if you know anything that can help big homie fill me in. I know these walls in here doing a lot of talking." Milly said

"From what I'm hearing, he rolling with the boy Wise from Lyons Ave and Aldine Ave, I figure he got word on the murder attempt on his life. When you left him down Yardville, he must feel you set it up or you left him for dead and now he wants some payback. I figure you at risk, the boys at risk and your girl at risk so you need to move extra careful."

"Young bull until he dead we going to all have to watch our backs and fronts, I need you to leave here call Night tell him to make sure Jahmela, Mela, the boys are all safe then y'all have to find G-Money" Uncle said.

"Alright, Uncle I'm on it now, stay up big homie" Milly said getting up pounding the glass and leaving the visit booth.

"Yo, Night what's up with that move you made today, did anything good come from it" Milly asked Night after he picked up the phone, Milly called Night as soon as he got out of the county and got his phone from the storage locker.

"Yeah I have something good but you know these phones, meet me at the spot in an hour" Night said.

Lockout sat in his hotel room across from Tesha trying to figure things out, he had been on the run with Tesha along time now. His cousin had set them up and now his money was getting low as he thought about what his next move had to be his mind went back to how he got away that night. His cousin tried to set him up, what saved him was his *alertness*.

When he left the room he realized he saw more white people than when he went in working off instincts he knew they were Feds. He slipped out a side door and texted Tesha, Plan B now he just had to hope Tesha was a real one and came through on her end. Plan b consisted of Tesha using a hammer Lockout kept in any car he was in to bust open the gas tank door on the next few cars parked nearby.

The next thing she would do is put a rag into the tanks and set them on fire and get low, as Lockout waited for the fireworks to start he was thinking she didn't come through. He had told her numerous times that if he ever texted her plan b it was the police closing in and he knew she could easily take the money he had in the car and just get low.

He was thinking she had done that but just as he tried to figure out what to do next, he heard the explosion and felt the ground shake. That's my rydah he said out loud to himself, he waited 5 minutes until he heard the sirens and in the commotion he got low.

Lockout took along pull of the garbage ass weed he had gotten in Buffalo; he was hiding out in Toronto, Canada. He figured he was closer to Canada and everybody ran to Mexico so they went north to the Six.

"Tesha you have to go get the money from my stash in the hood we running low and at this rate we can't go any longer without going to get the money. I got $ 180,000 stash in my mother basement nobody knows it's there but you know Tesha was a loyal Rydah but he was scared she would get the money and leave him high and dry. Ok bae I will be back tomorrow I love you stay in this room till I get back' Tesha said.

Clever woke up next to Leah he was fast approach 17 years old and becoming a man. He had already been accepted into Georgia Tech, and he had gotten an acceptance letter from Grambling University he wasn't sure where he wanted to go yet he like the idea of an HBCU but he loved Leah so as long as they were close he was cool. He hated that he was leaving Lil Rah and Tah but he wanted a future more than the hood, he thought about his father he knew he wanted revenge on his killer's Milly said some nigga name G-Money did it and to watch his back because G-Money might come for him too.

Clever wasn't a bitch but he wasn't a gangster either; he didn't know what to do should he go looking for G-Money. He knew what G-Money looked like from a picture Milly showed him other than that he knew nothing about G-Money. Lost in his thoughts Clever never notice Leah get up and head to the bathroom until he heard the shower cut on, Clever slipped out of bed and headed for the shower.

"Hey baby" he said as he slipped in the shower, he was a lucky young man, his mother gave him a lot of freedom, because he had earned it, he had the baddest girl in high school she 18 years old and he still was only 16 years old.

Her entered her from the back, stroked her a few times and was done before he even got started. Leah spoke up "what the hell was that boy".

"That shit too good, I owe you babe" Clever said to Leah.

They finished their shower got dressed and went to find the other two couples; they found them on the back patio. Sometime during the evening Aunt Gina had come home and to everyone's surprise she was sober in the kitchen cooking.

"Foods ready y'all come and get it" she yelled. They all headed to the kitchen Leah helped make plates while Tasha, Lil Rah's girl passed them out, most parents wouldn't accept their son's sleeping with girls under their roofs but Gina's wasn't like most parents. She was a fiend plus the girls kept the boys out of trouble.

"I need to talk to y'all" Gina said to the boys "And Since y'all here y'all can hear it too" She said to the girls. "I'm tired of the life I'm living I need better, you guys deserve better so first thing Monday morning I'm leaving to go to a 6 month detox and Rehab Center. I want to get clean I have to get clean, I love my family and I know I am losing y'all."

"Lil Rah and Tah you are going to stay with your Grandmother and Clever you have to go home, I know you guys don't want to go but I need y'all to understand this is going to help me focus on getting clean." Gina said to everyone.

Tah had heard the speech his mother had given them before and could careless he would believe it when he saw it. He had no intentions on going to his grandmother's house, he was going to dip before that ever happened but Lil Rah was happy.

"Okay Ma I'm proud of you, I got your back whatever you need I got you" Lil Rah said, Clever and the girls just shook their heads and remained silent.

Night had gotten word from Shonda, Wise's first baby mother that he was getting money with G-Money. Night already knew this but what she said next was worth the $2,500 he gave her, when he arrived that afternoon he couldn't lie for a thot with 4 kids she looked good. He started to get at her as his Lil man's started thinking but he pushed the thought out of his head.

"What's up? Shonda" Night asked her.

"Well hi to you too" she said "But anyway Wise been spending hell of bread, flossing all that shit but don't do shit for his kids, so one day I called him told him his son's need clothes and shit. He came over here gave me money then tried to get some pussy but before he could his phone rang.

He picked it up I could tell by the way he acted it was about money then I heard him say it's a go, they been here all weekend we can snatch all they asses. Can probably get like $50k a piece, he must've forgotten I was here because he said the boys and girls or just the boys. Once he realized I was there he stopped talking and said aight and hung up the phone.

I don't know what he was talking about then I found out y'all had money for any information about him and G-Money, nigga ain't shit anyway hope y'all do get him. So I can cash in this nigga insurance policy" Shonda said.

When Night met up with Milly he told him everything Shonda had told him, he even told him about her head game he wasn't there for that but after he got the information. Looking at her body his Lil man started talking again so he tired his luck.

"So what you think they got planned for tomorrow" Night asked.

"I can't be sure but it sound like some kidnapping ransom shit, the only real question is who they trying to snatch. We have until tomorrow to find out but a safe guess is they coming for our families." Milly said.

Chapter 27

(Beep, beep, beep) "Ma the van here, hurry up" Lil Rah yelled up the stairs.

"Boy, don't rush me I'm coming, I'm the parent in this motherfucker" Gina yelled down the stairs to her oldest son. Half joking, half serious it felt good to be getting back to her old self.

It was Monday morning and had been 3 whole days since she used, the urge to get clean came as she walked pass an UsWrld meeting and she heard from the Black Panther on the stage telling a story all too familiar. From that moment on she vowed to get clean and so far she was a success, she wound up staying for the whole speech.

Afterwards she asked the people about UsWrld, what they told her she liked and when they extended an olive branch. She reached out and grabbed if for dear life, now she was headed to rehab and her old life. She hoped she had went far away from her old self, she had heard Rah was in the county jail about to get his time reduced but she couldn't face him being the woman she had become.

She knew he and Jahmela were together but she couldn't be mad at that either, Jahmela had been his first love. Hell she even tried to help her get clean in the past, they deserved each other all she wanted was to be a mother again.

"Listen boys I need y'all to be good at grandma's house she loves both of you and can use the company. I will be gone 6 months but when I come back we will make up for lost time, I need y'all to stick together no matter what you are your brother's keeper y'all are all y'all have. And Clever keep up the good work I know about the college, watch over these two knuckleheads. I love y'all" Gina said to them.

"Okay Auntie I got you and you know I got them" Clever said.

(Beep, Beep) "Ma they beasting, I'm going to miss you when can you get visits" Lil Rah asked.

After the first 30 days she said as they walked out the door, when Tah saw the van he felt better. She was really going but he still wasn't going to his grandmother's house. "I love you Ma" Tah said.

"I Love y'all too be good your grandmother will be here when she gets off work" Gina said getting into the van.

Uncle sat in the back of the court room holding cell, dressed in a Blues Brothers suit with Salvatore Ferragamo shoes looking like money. His Lawyer had just came in the back and informed him that

195

everything was going according to plan, he would get his sentence reduced to 8 years with credit for the 54 months he had done already since he gotten arrested. He would only have 42 months left and it could be reduced to 26 months left with good behavior also his Lawyer said "We are still pushing to get it reduced to 7 years; you will be brought out in the next 15 minutes." Rosenberg said.

(Rashaan Anderson it's your times come on Uncle the bailiff said smiling.)

"Rashaan Anderson it has come to the states attention that you were illegally sentenced, your Lawyer's in your previous case dropped the ball. You signed for an 8 year plea and somehow where sentenced to 12 years, your Attorney Mr. Rosenberg has argued for a further sentence reduction to 7 years but you will not be getting that lucky today. We will only be correcting this miscarriage of Justice, you will be sentenced to 8 years in the U.S. Penitentiary with credit for the 54 months already served" Judge Raven said banging his gavel.

When Uncle got back to his tier it was 3pm he tried to call Jahmela, but her voicemail answered he got an eerie feeling but shook it off and decided to call back later.

"Yo, bruh what are you going to do, you going to stay at grandma house because I ain't with that shit. I'm glad momma going to get help but I ain't off going to grandma house" Tah said to his brother.

"I don't know Lil bruh I ain't feeling that shit either, you know grandma be on some extra strict shit. I love her but I am not off that at all but what we going to do" Lil Rah asked.

"I figured we can just stay here we just got to get low before grandma come that way we ain't here when she get here. I think she get off at 10pm tonight so we just got to be out before then" Tah said.

He watched as Gina left this morning in the van, it was only the second time he saw her since he had been watching Clever at her house, he could tell she was once a beautiful woman before the drugs. She talked to the kids before leaving in the van, he didn't know where she was going but from the look of the bags she had. She would be gone for a long time.

He was leaving tonight to go home, he really had no reason to be here right now but something had drawn him here. So as it was he sat behind the wheel of his rental Dodge Charger with limo tinted windows watching Gina leave her home, her sons, nephew and their girlfriends behind. They all stood there waving goodbye to her, he started to leave with the van, when he spotted the familiar Mazda van and decided to stay.

Just as it had done on previous times it rode through as if it was looking for something just wasn't right with that van. In fact the van was the only reason he was still in New Jersey.

Night and Milly had been out all night since Night got the information from Shonda about Wise. They were trying to figure out if G-Money was coming for Night's kids, Uncle's kids, both or neither he tried calling Clever but he wasn't answering. Milly thought he might be coming for his family since it seemed like the beef was personal, so he told Night.

"Look big bruh this shit seem personal between me and G-Money, so I need you to go home watch your family while I go find this nigga. If he want war I'm bring it to him not wait for him to come for me." Milly said.

"Naw young bull we ride together, I already took care of my family they good. We gone go get these niggas together, we get money together so we make niggas bleed together" Night responded.

"I have a plan anyway you still know where his baby mother stays at right" Night asked Milly.

"Yeah she live down Grafton Ave, but I was swinging through there the past few days haven't seen her yet" Milly told Night.

"Alright meet me down there in an hour, I got to get a few things" Night said.

As he made his way down to Grafton Ave he rode down 13th Street, he saw a familiar looking girl that's Tesha he thought. He pulled up on her, rolled his window down and yelled "Tesha, oh shit damn girl where the fuck you been at, what's good?"

"Ain't shit Milly same ole, same ole been chilling trying get my life together." Tesha said.

"Where the fuck Lockout been at, last I heard was y'all blew up a building or some shit in Ohio or something where trying to get away from the feds." Milly said.

"He is good; we ain't blown up shit nigga his cousin set him up. We had to get low but he good still trying duck them feds, I'm a tell him I saw you." Tesha told Milly.

"Naw, Naw tell that nigga to hit the burner phone a.s.a.p. it's a lot of shit done changed up out here but be safe Tesha I got to go, tell him I love that nigga." Milly said giving Tesha a hug.

"Alright Milly you already know be safe out here too I love you bruh" Tesha said to Milly hugging him back.

Milly left Tesha and headed down to Grafton Ave to meet up with Night. When he pulled up Night had switched up cars and brought out the van, as soon as Milly saw the van he knew Night had big plans.

"So what's the move my boy, I know you got big plans" Milly asked

"It's pretty simple he coming for us, so we come for him and anybody he coming with I got murder on my mind." Night said ready for whatever.

Chapter 28

G-Money and Wise were ready to make their move, they had been watching Clever and the rest of the kids for the past few days and tonight was go time. The Perfect night Uncle's wife had left and they could tell she would be gone a while, so she wasn't a concern. The time was now they would go in the house get the kids, call Milly and demand a ransom payment the plan was that simple cut and dry.

Wise pulled their car down a few houses from where they were going and killed the lights to watch the scene for a while.

"Truth or Dare Clever" Tasha asked.

"Truth" Clever answered.

"Is it true that Leah is pregnant" Tasha asked.

"I don't know about that you have to ask her that question" Clever responded.

"Okay it is your turn Leah are you pregnant" Mecca Tah's girl asked.

"No I am not pregnant, ain't nobody got time for that. I'm both to go to college that can wait." Leah said.

"Your turn Tah, Truth or Dare" **Leah asked.**

"Definitely Dare" Tah said.

"I dare you to tell Mecca the truth about how you feel about
her" Leah said.

"Mecca I fucks with you to the max to tell you the truth, I
really do like you. I don't know about know love shit but you definitely
the shit baby girl" Tah said.

"Aww that's so sweet come here baby" Mecca said kissing
Tah. "I fuck with you too boo."

They played a few more games; everybody got a Truth or
Dare question. They all laughed and joked throughout the night, they
all knew tonight might be the last night they chilled together like this
for a while in this house. So they made the most of it they enjoyed
every minute together, Tasha got up "I'm going to get something to
drink, y'all want something" Everybody put in their orders like Tasha
was a bartender.

Watching these growing teenagers you would've swore they
were grown ass men and women. They had all been through a whole lot
more that most children, Tasha and Mecca were 16 year old cousins
both raised by Mecca's mother who was now serving 25 years to life in
prison for murdering her boyfriend. When she found out he had been
raping her two children the past 3 years any chance he got.

Normally it would happen when she was at work but anytime she was outside of the house he would try also. She only was able to find out when she came home earlier one day and she noticed panties on the floor. She grew into a rage thinking he had the nerve to cheat on her in her own damn house. She was ready to fuck him and the bitch up, when she busted into the room and saw what was really going on she went damn near postal.

She went in her closest grab the gun she kept on the top shelf and started shooting, she shot until the gun was empty and just clicking. They moved in with Tasha's father after that all happened and they tried to visit her any chance they could but Tasha's father worked almost 7 days a week. So they rarely got the chance to go see her but they talked to her regularly.

Leah's story is a lot better; she had been raised by both parents who have been together since high school. They have been married now over 20 years, her mother was a Dental Assistant and her father owned, a Auto Mechanic shop for the past 8 years. They weren't rich or anything but they were better off than the average black family.

They were raising a good kid which was the main reason they gave Leah so much freedom, they didn't like Clever much but they trusted their daughter.

"Damn where is Tasha ass at, did she go to the store to get the drinks. Tasha girl were the hell you at" Leah yelled towards the kitchen.

G-Money was sitting in the van waiting for the night fall, so they could make their move they had maybe another 10-20 minutes before the darkness would totally set in. G-Money noticed the Dodge Charger parked close by but saw no one inside but with the tints all around he couldn't see the inside. Anyhow as night came he pulled into the driveway. They knew the kids were in the back of the house on the patio, as they got out of the van they headed to the front door.

As he sat in his car, he saw the van pull into Gina's driveway he saw two guys get out of the van and head to the front door. It looked like they were breaking into the house; he grabbed his gun and exited his vehicle following the two guys. Working with the night fall he couldn't make out the faces of either one of the two dudes.

As Wise broke into the front door followed by G-Money they could hear a girl saying something they couldn't really tell what she was saying though. Sounded like something about some drinks then they could hear others responding more clearly get me a soda. It was time the girl came into the house from the patio; Wise could see Tah facing towards them so they might be spotted by him.

Tasha had to walk past them to get to the kitchen, so they hid in the cut by the laundry room. When she walked past G-Money grabbed Tasha before she could yell Wise put the gun to her head and told her "Scream and you and everyone else dies". Wise pulled out some duct tape and taped he mouth then placed zip ties around her wrist and ankles.

Leah got up and headed towards the inside, she walked into the patio door just as Wise and G-Money put Tasha in the living room. Leah came walking in and yelled out "Tasha were you at, what you spiking our drinks girl" Leah was laughing as she walked into the living room. When she saw Tasha hog tied and the two men in the living room she let out a loud scream, she tried to run but G-Money caught her and clunked her in the head with his gun.

The kids on the porch all heard the scream, nobody knew why Leah was screaming but Tah's first reaction was to grab his gun. Which saved his life because just as he went to reach for his gun, on the table a bullet tore through the head rest of the chair he was sitting in?

As he made his way across the street, he could hear what sounded like gunshots inside the house. His first instinct was to run because in this white town the police would be showing up very soon, but he couldn't leave and if something happened to Clever without him helping that would kill him itself. So he ran across the street and entered the house staying low and in the shadows, he heard another shot and headed in that direction.

Night and Milly sat in the house of G-Money's baby mother waiting for her to come home, they looked around saw pictures or her and a little girl around 6 years old. Who was her exact mini me Milly couldn't lie, G-Money had picked a winner shorty was bad. As they searched the house looking for any clues as to her whereabouts Milly asked Night "so where you think she at, you think she knows anything".

Night's response was bone chilling "If she don't know anything when I'm done she gone be making up shit to tell us plus their lives depend on it" Night said pointing at the picture Milly was holding. Just as he put the picture down her house phone rung (Ring, Ring, Ring you reached Tonya sorry you couldn't reach me, I'm not home right now.)

As the person on the other end of the phone left a message, Milly could hear someone on the other side of the front door. He pointed at the door as he made eye contact with Night he mouthed "It's her". Night's phone started vibrating in his pocket; he hit the button to end the call and instantly it started vibrating again. With his gun in hand he pulled out his phone saw the caller id just as Tonya entered the apartment with a little girl. Milly surprised her with his gun "be quiet and you both live".

When Tah got to his gun he didn't waste any time to figure out shit, he saw the shot rip through the chair. He squeezed off 2 quick shots; he knew he hit something when he heard a muffled yelp. He didn't know who or how many people were coming for them but he wasn't going to do no running. Tasha and Leah were in there, he stopped shooting "Yo Clever you got your strap on you right". Tah asked his cousin.

"Yeah I got it on me but we can't just go barging in there though we need a plan" Clever said.

"Rah you don't have a gun so take Mecca out the back door to safety; me and Clever going to handle this but call Night and let him know what's going down." Tah said to his brother.

Clever ran to the front of the house looked in the window but couldn't see any of the people inside, so he went back to meet up with Tah.

"I can't see how many are in there" Clever said to Tah.

(Boom, boom) they heard the two shots and without planning anymore they were through the door. Clever could see one dude looking in the opposite direction; he opened fire hitting him once in the arm causing him to drop his gun. As Tah was about to run in that direction a shot came his way, he heard another shot then what sounded like something falling he returned fire with a volley of shots.

When Night saw the name on the caller id, Lil Rah on his phone he answered the phone "what's up Lil Rah I can't "(Boom) Night stopped what he was about to say as soon as he heard the gunshot on the other end of the phone. "Where you at Lil Rah, what was that, what's going on?"

"Night we at the house, somebody shooting at us I don't know what's going on but you need to get here." Lil Rah said to Night.

"Get out of the house I'm on my way" Night told Lil Rah "We got to go, I know where he at today's her lucky day" Night said to

Milly telling Tonya "Don't say nothing about any of this" then gave her a stack of money. Running out the door Milly pushed Tonya and ran behind Night.

"Who the fuck was that, what's good Night"? Milly asked once they got to the car.

"He at Gina house I'm pretty sure, that was Lil Rah he said somebody shooting at the kids at the house" Night told Milly.

Night jumped on Highway 21 headed to Union he made a regularly 30 minute trip in 12 minutes flat this was life or death situation fuck the police. Milly was out the passenger door before Night came to a complete stop in front of Gina's house. Night blocked the van in whoever was here definitely weren't going to live to need it anymore.

Milly got to the door about to enter the house when Night called out go to the back door, Milly ran to the backyard. Night was close behind once they got to the back door Night took the lead because he knew the layout of the house, Lil Rah had said they were on the back porch so he wanted to meet them there.

Night turned into a hallway and tripped over a body he instantly started putting bullets in the already died Wise.

When G-Money reached for his gun that had fallen when the bullet ripped through his arm, Tah let off a volley of shots that hit him in the chest as Tah continued to pull the trigger until his gun just checked he was out.

Clever could hear the sirens the cops would be here soon, he walked up to the bleeding would be kidnapper wearing a mask. He pulled the mask off and saw the face of the man Milly had showed him a picture of named G-Money. In rage and with the thoughts of his father's murder he shot him in the forehead and continued squeezing the trigger until Night grabbed his now empty gun and snapped him out of his trance.

Clever had just given G-Money his way out "that's for my father pussy". Milly picked up Tah's gun as he went to free Tasha and Leah who was bleeding from her side. The sirens grew closer "We have to get out of here now, Night before we go to jail."

"They need a story first there are two dead bodies in here" Night said noticing movement behind Milly he fired toward the back door hitting Two5 in the leg as he tried to escape.

"Look it's 4 of y'all in here and she shot they are going to believe whatever y'all say. So tell them somebody broke in here there was a struggle one of y'all got the gun in the process and started shooting." Milly said.

They ran out of the front door jumped into the car and left just as the police pulled on the block. Night and Milly were just able to escape, this shit was crazy but the boys held their own and made it out alive they just would have to convince the police of the story now. Uncle didn't know who he shot at, at the back door but G-Money and Wise were dead now he would try and find out who the other person was.

The police pulled up to the house the kids were outside waiting for them they had gone over the story a few times and felt like it would work. When the officers got out of their cars they walked up to the kids notice the girl bleeding and called for the ambulance.

"Hello kids what's going on here, we received a call of shots fired at this location" the officer asked the kids.

Clever took the lead "Yes officer me, my cousins, and our girlfriends were home sitting on the back porch talking and hanging out. One of the girls got up to get some drinks for everyone, she went in the house to get them but she never came back out. So my girlfriend Leah went to see what was taking her so long, once she got in the house we heard her scream." Clever said before continuing.

"So we went into the house to see why she was screaming that's when we got into a fight with the men that broke into the house. In the middle of the scuffle the man dropped his gun causing it to go off after that we all tried to get the gun. I came up with it

211

and fired at the man hitting him that's when another man came from no were we got into a gun battle and we won." Clever said

"On young man where are these men at now, did they leave or are they still in the house" the officer asked Clever.

"No sir they didn't getaway they are in the house bleeding I think we killed them though I'm not sure I never seen a dead body sir" Clever said faking it for the officer.

"Okay young man thank you for your help we will go in and see what's going on, Officer Robinson watch these kids while we go in the house there has been a shooting possible multiple dead inside the house" the lead Officer Johnson told his partner.

Upon entering the house the officers walked into a blood bath they noticed to dead men on the floor shot multiple times, they wonder how some 15 or 16 year old kids could do this to grown men. But they accepted the kids story after seeing the men they called for the coroner, interviewed the kids again. They were satisfied with the story so there would be no need to investigate further.

Chapter 29

2 years later..

Uncle was a short timer now he only had a few more weeks left before his upcoming release date, as he sat in his cell he thought about his life and the last two years. He thought about everything that had happened since the night at his house, he flashbacked to when he heard about what went down.

Breaking News, Breaking News, News Channel 12 reporting live from Union, N.J. This is Melissa Ford we are live on the scene of a home invasion, attempted abduction, turned murder. All we can say now is they the victims appear to be juveniles and will not be identified but from information reported to us the kids where at home alone hanging out waiting on their grandmother to arrive.

When 2 or more suspects broke into their front door of the home taped up a few of them, then there was a struggle ending in 2 of the suspects being shot one dead on arrival. The other suspect is in crucial condition; let's go to the Union township Police Chief. He will be coming to address us and give us a live briefing.

Uncle was tuned in as soon as he heard something about Union, N.J. and as the camera man panned to in on the area where the Chief would be appearing soon. He saw the house where the shooting took place and when he saw his house he stopped caring about the news and ran to the phones he called everybody. First he called Jahmela, then Kamela, Night and Milly nobody answered so he kept trying to call until he realized they weren't going to pick up.

He went back to the TV to watch the rest of the News Conference, the Police Chief was speaking. Uncle listened once he heard one 18 year old female was shot in the hip but was in stable condition and that the other kids in the house were unharmed he left the TV room. Went back to the phones and tried to make another call, he got the same results.

Next he did the best thing he could in a time like this and went into his cell and prayed to Allah. After he was finished praying he tried to call once again this time Night answered his phone. Once Night accepted the call Uncle went in "What's good Bruh I saw the news what's up out there".

"I can't really say much big bruh but that problem we been having is over, tried to make a move on our young bulls but they were too Clever, Rah" Night said using codes. "When we finally realized what was going on, we got there as soon as possible but the situation

214

was already handled. But the crazy shit is I think Two5 was there too and help the young bulls to end on of the pest for them."

"Alright bruh let me get off this phone, love that nigga" Uncle said. He felt a lot better knowing everybody was safe.

Snapping out of his daydream he had a lot going on now he and Jahmela were engaged to be married, Clever had moved to Atlanta and was now a freshman in College, and Lil Rah was a senior in High School with plans to follow Clever to College. Tah had even changed some and was doing better he wasn't on his way to College or anything.

Tah was a gangster at heart and was now hustling for Milly but at least he kept his mother clean and took care of her. He even visited Uncle from time to time, Milly had become a true boss now and the streets feared him and Night. Kamela had moved to Florida with her new husband everything was good well almost Lockout was still alive and on the run.

Their only real problem was that Two5 was still out there somewhere and Uncle just couldn't let that go. He had to sentence Two5 to the same fate of his brother and he was dying to know, why he saved the kids. Yeah he would definitely catch up with Two5 he only had a few weeks left and a bullet had Two5's name on it already.

Uncle had Night on Two5 ass looking high and low for him but as of now Two5 was a ghost. Night figured Two5 had to be out of the city because he had a lot of bread on that man's head and he knew niggas would cash in on that if they saw Two5. They streets had been in a frenzy the past 2 years everybody was getting locked up by the Alphabet boys, the city had the DEA, FBI, ATF and Newark PD on ever none hustler.

Uncle knew Milly and Night where keeping a low profile with all the heat coming down on the city but he also knew they still had to eat. So he came up with the idea of them taking their operation on the road and it was a great idea because it was the main reason the Feds hadn't gotten them yet.

Everyone was awaiting Uncle's return to the streets when he went away he was a legendary king fair to everyone. He was paying all his workers fair exchange and he never thought about being a snake to anyone his brother's death was pain staking but he held down his family just as he was supposed to do. He was a boss of all boss and the streets would treat him as such upon his return to the free world. He dozed off in his cell ready for his upcoming freedom.

Chapter 30

Two5 made it out the back door just as Night saw him and sent a shot at him hitting him in the leg, he wasn't there to hurt the kids so he just limped away jumped in his car and sped away. He had a girl who was a Nurse he call Inayah and told her he had been shot and need her help, she told him to come to her house now before he bleed out.

Two5 had been watching the kids from a distance for the past few weeks; ever since Ray had been murdered he was back in Jersey staying low from the heat down in Atlanta. He felt great watching the kids he felt connected with Clever he really wanted to protect them since he had been seeing the van hang around he was watching them extra close.

He had no idea what or who was in the van or what the van was trying to do but he would watch them extra closely. If anything went down he would definitely be there to hold the kids down.

Two5 pulled up too Inayah house bleeding like crazy, he parked his car jumped out and headed for her front door. He rang her bell a few times before he heard her coming down the stairs; she opened the door without asking who it is. She answered the door

"Two5 what the fuck going on get in here, let me get you right nigga fuck you doing now I thought u stop that bullshit." Inayah said

"Girl I ain't into none that bullshit no more I was trying to help some kids, and things got crazy but anyway help a nigga out before I bleed to death." Two5 said.

Inayah told Two5 to go to her bathroom while she when to get some supplies, she had her a nice amount of Nursing item in her room she always kept this stuff on hand just for matters like this one. She ran in her room got some gauges, some towels, scissors and some stitches. She didn't know what Two5 had gotten himself into this time but her knowing him it was some bullshit.

As she got the items and went back into the backroom blood was all over, she told him to take the towel and hold pressure on his leg as she cut his pants off it looked like this was only place he was hit, as she got his pants off it was a lot of blood but it didn't look that bad the bullet had went straight through and didn't hit an artery.

She told him to bite down on another towel before she poured the alcohol on his leg "this going to burn Two5" she poured the alcohol all over his leg then started cleaning his womb, she made a tourniquet to slow down the bleeding before she stitched up his womb. Once she got the bleeding to slow down enough she stitched up his leg, she wound up giving him 9 stitches but he would survive.

"You good boy you will live now tell me the truth what the fuck you done got into chance I help you I need to know not trying to be you co-defendant." Inayah said.

"Girl know its best you don't know what happen, you already know I'm a stand up nigga you ain't got to worry about nothing coming back to you. But I will tell you I helped some kids nigga was trying to kill or some shit. Thank baby girl you a lifesaver, here take this" Two5 said giving Inayah a wad of cash.

"I gotta go but I will call you once I figure out what the fuck is really going on, I almost died I need answers" Two said before getting up and limping to the door.

Inayah just looked at him because she didn't know where he was going with a bloody shirt and no pants on "Two5 that's all good but first you need some clothes to put on sit you as down let me get you some of my man clothes at least genius." Inayah said to him.

Two5 was so focused on figuring out what the fuck was going on his totally forget he was damn near naked "Oh damn my bad boo yeah do that for me"

Inayah brought Two5 the clothes she found "I don't know if you can fit this but it's better than what you got on now" She told him handing him the clothes.

"Thank you love it's going to have to do, I don't have a better option right now. I really appreciate you I will always remember what you did for me." Two said getting dressed and ready to get out of there and get his ear to the streets, he didn't know who made the move on the kids but he knew who the kids where and he knew Uncle and Night would be on a war path too, Uncle was still locked up but he had plenty of reach in the streets.

As Night and Milly made their escape they wanted to know who the fuck got out of that back door, Night wasn't 100 percent sure but it looked like Two5. He couldn't understand what went down because it looked like the dude was trying to help the kids, the more he thought about it but he had no idea why Two5 would do that. He didn't know exactly what was going on but he and Milly would wage war on the streets of Jersey until they got some answers that was a fact.

"Milly I think that was Two5 that ran out the back door bruh, I don't know why that nigga was their but I think he was trying help the kids because there is no way they would have made it against 3 grown as killers that for sure." Night said.

"I don't either big bruh but you already know how I'm giving it up, the kids my family so who ever bring a move on them they got to die. I'm going to pull up on every nigga, on every block in the city until we find out who ran out that back door." Milly said meaning every word.

"Okay young bull you already know the shit, but first we got to go check on Mela and Jahmela, once we let them know that they have to go check on the kids we can ride out." Night said

Two5 was on a mission he couldn't figure out what happened but the streets where up in frenzy everyone heard what happened to the kids. Night and Milly where on a mission that were trying to find out about him they didn't know for sure it was him but they thought it was so he was staying low but he knew eventually they would cross paths, so he decided it might be his best option to reach out to them before they found him. He knew it would be dangerous he was the cause of Haz death and he killed Ray.

He was still healing from his gunshot wounds so what every he decided to do it would have to wait until he was 100% because if things went wrong he need to be able to protect himself.

Chapter 31

Once Night got in touch with Jahmela, and let her know what went down she called Kamela and they got in touch with their lawyer and headed toward the police station. They didn't want the police to try and question the kids and get them to say anything wrong. When they arrived at the 5th precinct their lawyer Rosenberg was already their awaiting on them. They said hi to him and headed inside they knew they had to stop the conversion as soon as possible.

Kamela walked to the receptionist and informed her, they were looking for Clever Anderson and the rest of the boys. The officer asked them to wait while she went and got the Detective handling the case. About 5 minutes later the officer came back with the Detective Roundtree, he walked up and introduced himself to the lawyer, Kamela and Jahmela.

He informed them what the boys told them and happened, than he told them they weren't question the boys and more and had been waiting on their parents to arrive so they go home. Kamela thanked the officer and asked him where the boys where at, the Detective told the desk officer to go get the young men and bring them to out to their family. Next the lawyer asked him to speak privately while the women waited for the boys to be brought out.

"Yes hello Detective I am the boys Attorney Mr. Rosenberg I heard what you told the ladies but I would like to know all the details to the situation. I know you said the boys where in the clear as to this was self-defense but as there Attorney I just want to make sure nothing comes down on them later on down the line Sir."

"Okay Mr. Rosenberg I can respect that, you are looking out for the best interest of your clients but I can assure you from the statement the boys gave us it was a self-defense situation. We will finish our investigation in the next few days and you are welcome to some and get the police report once we are finished but as of the situation everything looks legit some guys broke into their house and tried to kidnap the kids but they were able to fight back and kill the men with their own weapons." Detective Roundtree told the boys Lawyer.

The boys came out ran to their family hugging and kissing them, the boys had been at the precinct about 5 hours. The cops had questioned them but they believed the story they will told so the cops and left them alone and where waiting for their guardians to arrive so they could send them home. Kamela thank the officers and they all walked outside with their Lawyer.

Once they got outside their Lawyer told Kamela and Jahmela what the Detective told him, he was sure nothing would come of this but he told them he would come next week and get the full police report and contact them once he had it. He told the boys they did a great job and to be careful just in case the police came around looking for any more information. He shook everybody hands and walked toward his car.

Kamela asked the boys what happened once they got to the car, the boys told them the full story of events. It sounded like a movie or some shit Kamela and Jahmela were will trained in the streets after being with Uncle and Haz all these years but this was different someone had come to their home and tried to harm the boys. They were glad the boys made and killed the dudes but something had to change plus they knew Uncle, Night, and Milly wouldn't rest until they found the other dude that got away the streets were about to be crazy.

Present Day...

Things were getting back to normal now; Clever had moved to Atlanta and was attending Spelman College. Him and Leah were both

224

going according to plan they were sharing and apartment and both attending Spelman and Lil Rah was now a senior in High School and planning on going to Atlanta also for college. Tah was still going off in the streets of Newark but he had slowed down the drama and was just getting money now.

Uncle had just called Clever and told him he got his date and would be coming home soon, everyone was happy about hear the news. Clever planned on going home for a few days to see Uncle once he was released. Tah kept him informed on the street shit going on in Newark, they had found out that it was Two5 his father old friend that helped them that day in the house.

He heard that his father was setup by Two5 but he didn't know all the details about what had really happened, Night and Milly were still looking for Two5 but nobody had heard anything on him lately. Since he had been in Atlanta he visited Ray's old Club it was still the spot to be, he even might Ray's old business partner a few times once Kevin heard he was Ray's family he showed the boy mad love everything was on the Club anytime he and his college friends went there.

Leah said she didn't like the dude he seemed sketchy to her but Clever had no issue with the dude but he always kept his eyes on Kevin. He didn't know what happened to his Cousin but he was going

225

to try and find out he didn't have the street cred down here so it wasn't going to be easy he knew that. He found out that Kevin was from Newark to so he figured he would have Tah or Night run a check on the dude.

Night and Milly here still looking for Two5 they had found out a lot of information about Two5 over the past two years the streets had finally confirmed that Two5 setup the robbery that killed Haz. So they were really beasting now to try and find Two5 they always thought he played a part in the setup but now with confirmation they knew he had to die but it was like he was a ghost over the past for years. Night had heard he was down south somewhere but had no idea where he was at.

He got a call from Tah one night asking about some dude in Atlanta named Kevin Lockette that was Ray's business partner on a Club before Ray was murder. He didn't know a Kevin Lockette from Newark but Tah said Clever had called him asking about the dude so Tah was trying to find out who the nigga was and if anything was good with son. Night told him he would check into it and see if he came up with anything he would hit him back once he found out something.

"Alright Night just let me know I'm going to keep checking on it too, I don't know why Clever want to know but you know him it got to be a reason." Tah said to his Uncle Night.

Tah hung up with Night and called Clever back "what's good cuzzo I just got off phone with Night I told him what you wanted to know he said he going to check into it, but you already know I'm still on it as soon as I know something I'm hit your phone" Tah said.

"Aight cuzzo good looking I love that nigga, as soon as you find out anything let me know cause I think dude man on some bullshit I just don't know what it is but that shit with Ray don't seem right to me." Clever said before hanging up.

A week later Clever got a call from Uncle he had been still trying to figure that shit out about this nigga Kevin.

"What's good nephew how things going down there, how's Leah?' Uncle asked

"Everything good Uncle, we out here living enjoying this school thing. I got a question for you though I went to the Club Ray had down here a couple times shit lit but anyway I met his old business partner dude seem cool but I heard he from Newark too so I had Tah and Night trying to find out about dude. So far they ain't find out shit about him though." Clever said to Uncle.

"Oh yeah why you want to know about dude if you say he cool" Uncle asked

"I don't know yet but that shit with Ray don't seem right and dude took a liking to me and I want to know if he on some fuck shit." Clever said

"Oh aight nephew better safe than sorry that's a fact so what do you need to know, what's this dudes name I'm see what I can find out" Uncle said to Clever.

"Alright Uncle I just need find out what this nigga reputation is, is he a stand up dude he offered me a job at the club so I need to know what he about and once I found out he from Newark I figured it could be possible. His name is Kevin Lockette." Clever told Uncle.

"Hold on nephew you said the nigga name is Kevin Lockette, what this dude looks like I might know exactly who this dude is." Uncle said to Clever a little bit excited this might be a man he had been looking for some years now.

"He is like 6 foot 2 inch tall stocky dark skinned dude with a beard and a bald head" Clever told Uncle.

Uncle listened to Clever he had seen Two5 in years so he really didn't know if that was him but the name Clever said was definitely his name. Uncle thought about everything Clever told him then it hit him Night and Milly said they thought Two5 helped the kids that day so he figured he could give Night the description Clever gave him and find out was it really Two5.

"Nephew, watch out for that dude it sounds like it might be an old friend of me and your father but let me get in touch with Night and Milly. Once I talk to them I will call you back and find out exactly who this dude is but until this watch out for him. If it is who I think it is he is a very dangerous man." Uncle said to Clever thinking only of what this could really mean.

"Okay Uncle I got you I'm a watch out for dude and stay away from him for now until I hear from you." Clever said to Uncle before ending their conversation.

Uncle called Night right away after hanging up with Clever but Night didn't answer so he called Milly next but he didn't answer either. He thought about calling Kamela and Jahmela but he didn't want to alarm them in case it wasn't Two5 but he was pretty sure it had to be. He went back to his cell he would call Night and Milly tomorrow until he spoke to them.

Clever didn't know what to think once he got off the phone with Uncle, at first Uncle sounded happy about find out about dude then he changed in a blink of an eye and was telling him to be careful. He didn't know what was going on but he always listened to Uncle so he would be extra careful about being around dude until he found out what Uncle knew. He told Leah about his conversation with Uncle, she just shook her head and told him to be careful also.

Uncle got in touch with Night the next morning, he told him everything Clever told him the night before. Night was amazed it sounded like it was Two5 he remember the dude that ran out the back door was a tall stocky bald headed dude. Night was in a rage he wanted to go down to Atlanta and just go kill the nigga but Uncle told him to wait he would be home in a week and he wanted to do it personally now that they had the drop of Two5. It was like a god send he was coming home and they finally had the information they had been looking for the past few years.

"Alright Rah you already know I'm going to wait for you to come home but this shit got to be done as soon as possible." Night said to Uncle.

"You already know brother let Milly know what the fuck going on and put together everything that's the first thing we doing when I get home, love that nigga let me call Clever and let him know what's going on." Uncle told Night.

Uncle hung up with Night and called Clever but he didn't answer, he figured he must be in class, so he went back to his cell he would call back later. He got to his cell all smiles he finally knew where the nigga that set his brother up was and he was coming home next week payback would be swift and painful.

Clever saw the call from Uncle but he was in class and couldn't pick up he figured Uncle must have found out what he wanted to know. He knew Uncle would call him back later so he just finished his classes for the day and awaited what Uncle had to tell him if she was funny with oh boy he was going to kill him. He wasn't a killer but he just knew something was fishy with dude and his family and he wanted payback fuck this school shit right now.

Tah was out all night trying to find out about the nigga Kevin in Atlanta but he couldn't come up with anything. He was talking to one of his homeboys when a black car pulled up on them rolled their window down ask for some weed, when his homie went to make the sell a gun came out the window and fired 6 or 7 shots at them then sped off. Before Tah could even shot back the car sped off and his homie was down on the ground bleeding, Tah ran to him he was bleeding bad but he was still breathing Tah ran to his car and pull up to his homie threw him in the car and sped to the hospital.

Shit was crazy Tah had never saw the car before and didn't know if the shots were for him or his homie, he had a gun in his car so he couldn't just go to hospital so he pulled up took homie out the car laid him in front of emergency doors and ran back to his car and sped off. He didn't know what that was but he definitely was going to find out, Clever shit had to wait right now niggas tried to kill him and his homie might not make it.

His next move was to call Lil Rah and let him know what happened, Lil Rah wasn't in the street but nigga knew they were brothers so he needed him to know to be on point. Next he called Milly and let him know what just went down, Milly told him to pull up on him so they could figure out what shit was before he did anything crazy.

Uncle had finally gotten back in touch with Clever what he had to tell Clever he had to be extra careful because all the phone calls were recorded but it was of the upmost importance that Clever knew who he was dealing with.

"What's up nephew how are things going today, I found out some important information on that club and it's not a good business deal." Uncle said to Clever.

"Ok Uncle what the reason the deal is bad" Clever asked already knowing something was fishy with oh boy because Uncle was talking in code and it could be only one reason for that.

"Listen nephew him and dude that knew your father is one and the same person, he was at the house with you and the kids one day and things went wrong. I don't know exactly why he wants to be a business partner of yours but don't deal with him. I knew him back in the day he was a good business man but he was only worried about himself." Uncle said hope Clever knew what he was saying.

"Ok Uncle I hear you loud and clear I won't go into business with him, I always listen to what you say and I know exactly what you are saying" Clever said to Uncle already forming a plan. He knew what Uncle was saying this was the dude Two5 that played a part in his father downfall, Clever understood the danger of this dude but he was thinking only one thing; Revenge.

"Ok nephew I will call you back tomorrow but I need you to do one thing and that is nothing. No business to nothing." Uncle said before hang up.

Clever sat back thinking of his next move, he knew Uncle would be mad if he made a move on dude but in his heart of hearts he couldn't just let this rest. He would wait a few days and arrange a sit down meeting with Two5 and do his in plain and simple. Uncle would just have to be mad this time.

Tah pulled up on Milly about an hour later, he jumped out the car barely putting it in park. He was on fire he couldn't believe somebody would try to move on him and his people broad daylight. He had too much respect in the streets plus with Milly, Night and his father he just didn't think he could be touched.

"What's good young boy, what the fuck happened I need all the information you can remember" Milly said to Tah.

"Big bruh I don't know what the fuck happened, I pulled up on one my homies on the block. We was kicking it then nigga in a Black Charger pulled up asked for some bally. When my man went to make the sale I saw an arm come out and start shooting I yelled to son to watch out then went to pull my strap and shot back but they murked off a.s.a.p. When I saw my homie fall I ran to him threw him in the car and sped to the hospital, I dropped him off at the emergency room and sped off before cops came." Tah told Milly what he remembered.

"Young boy did you notice anybody following you today or last couple days, do you recognize the car or anybody in the car. Do

234

you know anything about a nigga you had a beef with trying to come for you anything you know can help us on this one." Milly said to him.

"Not really bruh I seen the car before but it's a bunch them shits in the hood, and as far as the niggas in car I ain't see no faces or nothing. I ain't had no beefs since the shit at the skating rink I just been on my get money shit." Tah told Milly.

"Alright Lil bruh I'm call Night let him know what went and so we can put our ear to the streets, once we find out who made the move you already know the outcome." Milly said meaning every word.

"Okay big bruh, if I hear anything on my end you going to be the first to know. I ain't making know move until you and Night let me know what it do." Tah said giving Milly dap.

Clever had been planning his move for the past 3 days he had setup the meeting with Two5 and it was scheduled for tomorrow Friday afternoon. Clever plan was simple he would come with his man from Brooklyn that was in school with him, he would talk business with Two5. Before long he would bring up Newark and his father and see what Two5 did if he didn't like his answers he would shoot him right there in his office. Tomorrow would be a big day and no mistakes

235

could be made this was a life or death situation Clever knew and he had every idea of being the one to come out alive.

Uncle was sitting in his cell thinking about everything he had 4 days left, he could taste his freedom now. He didn't call home anymore or even leave his cell his was focused on his mission. He had to get at Two5 and then take back his crown, he thought about leaving the streets behind but he knew before he could do that he had to fix everything that was fucked up first.

Uncle knew what happened to his son Tah, he was a little concerned about what he would do but his biggest concern was Clever. He knew Clever was a smart kid but Two5 was the one that set his father up and sometimes emotions take over. He prayed to Allah to protect his family that was all he could do at the present time until he touched down.

Friday had come and it was time for Clever to meet up with Two5, he had gone over his plan a thousand times. He would trap Two5 into admitting who he was and what he did to not only his father but Ray also if Two5 tried to deny what he had done he would just shot him get up and walk out. But if Two5 wanted to talk he would listen and then kill him after he knew he had the element of surprise so he felt confident in his plan plus he knew his Brooklyn homie was with the shit.

Clever called Two5 and told him he would be there with in the next 30 minutes, Two5 really liked the young boy style he was a smart, hustler. He had been watching him for a few years and knew that he had no idea who he really was, he thought about the past around the kid. He always thought that he was his real father but Kamela switched up on him and started fucking with Haz as soon as he got locked up.

That hurt him so much sitting in jail knowing that Haz had his life, his wife and maybe his son he couldn't take it. So the first chance he got to set Haz up he had to do it, he didn't want them to kill Haz though he wanted to do that personally but first he had to get his money up when he came home. But they fucked up and not only killed Haz but almost killed Kamela that's why Rock had to die he was stupid and stupidity is dangerous.

He had big plans for Clever he was going to let him run the club while he was in college, so that he could keep a close eye on him and get to know him. He figured if Clever was his real son once he found out he would accept him and they could become friends at the least. But he made one missed calculation Clever almost died that night too and he would never forget that.

Clever pulled up in a brand new Audi A6 dressed to the nines in an all-black Armani Suit, Salvatore Ferragamo Shoes. Clever looked like the ultimate business man not just a college kid from the ghetto of Newark and his man Brooklyn was just as sharp. They both checked there silenced 9mm pistols then Clever called Two5 and let him know he was outside. Two5 said come in the building and come up stairs to his office.

They had gone over the plan too many times Clever would introduce Brooklyn to Two5 and then they would sit down and talk. Clever walked up the stairs Brooklyn right by him, he knocked on Two5's office door he heard him say come in.

"What's going on with you young men, how are you guys today, y'all looking like a million bucks I see" Two5 said shaking each man's hand.

"Hello how are you doing Kevin this is my classmate William Johnson, he is a trusted friend of mind and if I going to work with you. I want you to know him because he will be able to help me." Clever said introducing the two men.

"Hello sir how are you doing it is a pleasure to meet you" William said shaking Kevin's hand firmly he knew the biggest sign of respect is looking a man eye to eye and having a strong handshake.

"Have a seat gentleman; let's talk business I had a proposition for Clever but if you are a friend of his then you are a friend of mine. Here's what I had in mind for you guys since y'all are still in school this will be a part-time paid internship, I have quite a few businesses and I don't plan on running this club forever so I'm looking to take someone under my wings.

I will show you both the ropes of the club business, but what I need from you guys now is basically shadow me. You guys will learn the business of buy the alcohol dealing with the girls. The business bank accounts and basically anything else you will need to know to become successful businessmen in the future." Two5 said smiling paying attention to their reaction.

Clever cleared his throat and spoke up "Listen that sounds good to me, sounds like an opportunity for me and my man to really learn something and I respect you so I really appreciate the chance to prove myself. I just have a few questions before me go into business. How do you feel about this opportunity Will?" Clever, asked his man before finishing with the rest of his question.

"It sounds good to make we can get paid and learn some shit, I ready when you read" Will said actually liking the plan but knowing they were here for a reason. "Before we go any further though can I go to the bathroom" Will said giving the sign he and Clever agreed on.

"Yeah young boy it's down the hall to the right, 3 doors down. When you come back we can do the applications and finish up the business." Kevin said; ready to work with the young men.

When Will left out of the office Clever started up with his questioning.

"Mr. Lockette I respect you and I appreciate the opportunity but what made you choose me out of everyone in Atlanta?" Clever asked.

"Well Clever the day I met you and you told me you were Ray's cousin I automatically felt the urge to show you some of the things. He showed me before his untimely death, I saw you in him he was a go getter and I saw that in you" Two5 responded.

"Okay cool how did you meet my cousin anyway you know he was from Newark, just like me so what brought y'all together?" Clever asked pulling his gun from his waist and putting it on his lap out of Two5's view.

"There was one day I saw I'm in a restaurant talking to someone it look like he really didn't want to be dealing with. Once the guy left I walked over to him and we spoke and found out we could be of help to each other and from there over business relationship took off." Two5 said telling the truth.

"Okay that's understandable so where, are you originally from Mr. Lockette are you from Atlanta or somewhere else?" Clever asked ready to get it over with but he knew to stick to the plan to keep Two5 off guard.

"Actually I'm originally from Newark as well that was one of the reasons me and Ray clicked up instant. We were both from up top and with all these county niggas down here you have to be careful. Got a lot of haters down here because we from up north." Two5 said really getting annoyed of the 21 questions but he was wondering what was taking Will so long.

Will had walked down toward the bathroom and then circled back and was standing outside the door waiting to hear Clever ask the question that would signal him to bust into the office. He knew Clever's question so he knew it was about 3 questions away.

"So what brought you down here to Atlanta, not trying to be all in your business but were you on the run or something if we going to do business I need to know my danger level?" Clever said, gaming Two5.

"No I wasn't on the run young man; I just saw a better opportunity down here in Atlanta. So I made the move and it has been a great decision. Listen Clever I respect you but we can stop the 21 question and get down to business where is Will he been in bath a while. Two5 said.

Clever knew Will was at the door and since Two5 had just said what he did it was time to get the show on the road, fuck the Questioning.

"Okay Mr. Lockette just one more question and we can get down to business" Clever said grabbing his pistol off his lap and pulling it on Two5 just as Will came busting through the door.

Two5 was caught totally off guard but he wasn't surprised he figured Clever was too smart not to put two and two together.

"Hold on Clever what's going on here, I thought we were friends I just what's to help you two young men." Two5 said trying to by sometime they had the drop on him and he was alone, he had to figure something out.

"Fuck all that bullshit Mr. Lockette or should I say Two5. Nigga you killed my father, almost killed my mother and me plus probably Ray man save the bullshit. Now sit the fuck down before I just shoot your stupid as now let's talk nigga." Clever said.

Two5 looked defeated he knew that if Clever knew all that information there wasn't away he was going to make it out of this situation. But truth, be told he at least owed the young man a conversation maybe he could change his mind but he would do no

242

begging for his life. He was a real gangster OG and he was off that shit. He sat down crossed his legs and said okay young niggas let's talk.

To be Continued...